PUFFIN BOO

Escape from

MR LEMONCELLO'S
LIBRARY

CHRIS GRABENSTEIN is the #1 *New York Times* bestselling author of many books, as well as the co-author of numerous fun and funny page-turners for young readers with James Patterson. Chris lives in New York City with his wife J.J., two cats and a dog named Fred.

Visit chrisgrabenstein.com for trailers, preview chapters, bonus puzzles and more!

The Mr Lemoncello series by Chris Grabenstein:

ESCAPE FROM MR LEMONCELLO'S LIBRARY
MR LEMONCELLO'S LIBRARY OLYMPICS
MR LEMONCELLO'S GREAT LIBRARY RACE

Escape from MR LEMONCELLO'S LIBRARY

CHRIS GRABENSTEIN

PUFFIN

PUFFIN BOOKS

UK | USA | Canada | Ireland | Australia
India | New Zealand | South Africa

Puffin Books is part of the Penguin Random House group of companies
whose addresses can be found at global.penguinrandomhouse.com.

www.penguin.co.uk
www.puffin.co.uk
www.ladybird.co.uk

First published in the United States by Random House
Children's Books, New York, 2013
Published in Great Britain by Puffin Books 2017

001

Text copyright © Chris Grabenstein, 2013
Cover art copyright © Gilbert Ford, 2013

The moral right of the author has been asserted

Printed in Great Britain by Clays Ltd, St Ives plc

A CIP catalogue record for this book is available from the British Library

ISBN: 978–0–141–38766–6

All correspondence to:
Puffin Books
Penguin Random House Children's
80 Strand, London WC2R 0RL

For the late Jeanette P. Myers,
and all the other librarians who help us find
whatever we're looking for

1

This is how Kyle Keeley got grounded for a week.

First he took a shortcut through his mother's favourite rosebush.

Yes, the thorns hurt, but having crashed through the brambles and trampled a few petunias, he had a five-second jump on his oldest brother, Mike.

Both Kyle and his big brother knew exactly where to find what they needed to win the game: inside the house!

Kyle had already found the pinecone to complete his "outdoors" round. And he was pretty sure Mike had snagged his "yellow flower". Hey, it was June. Dandelions were everywhere.

"Give it up, Kyle!" shouted Mike as the brothers dashed up the driveway. "You don't stand a chance."

Mike zoomed past Kyle and headed for the front door, wiping out Kyle's temporary lead.

Of course he did.

Seventeen-year-old Mike Keeley was a total jock, a high school superstar. Football, basketball, baseball. If it had a ball, Mike Keeley was good at it.

Kyle, who was twelve, wasn't the star of anything.

Kyle's other brother, Curtis, who was fifteen, was still trapped over in the neighbour's yard, dealing with their dog. Curtis was the smartest Keeley. But for *his* "outdoors" round, he had pulled the always unfortunate Your Neighbor's Dog's Toy card. Any "dog" card was basically the same as a Lose a Turn.

As for why the three Keeley brothers were running around their neighbourhood on a Sunday afternoon like crazed lunatics, grabbing all sorts of wacky stuff, well, it was their mother's fault.

She was the one who had suggested, "If you boys are bored, play a board game!"

So Kyle had gone down into the basement and dug up one of his all-time favourites: Mr Lemoncello's Indoor-Outdoor Scavenger Hunt. It had been a huge hit for Mr Lemoncello, the master game maker. Kyle and his brothers had played it so much when they were younger, Mrs Keeley wrote to Mr Lemoncello's company for a refresher pack of clue cards. The new cards listed all sorts of different bizarro stuff you needed to find, like "an adult's droopy underpants", "one dirty dish", and "a rotten banana peel".

(At the end of the game, the losers had to put everything back exactly where the items had been found. It was an official rule, printed inside the top of the box, and made winning the game that much more important!)

While Curtis was stranded next door, trying to talk the neighbour's Doberman, Twinky, out of his favourite tug toy, Kyle and Mike were both searching for the same two items, because for the final round, all the players were given the same Riddle Card.

That day's riddle, even though it was a card Kyle had never seen before, had been extra easy.

FIND TWO COINS FROM 1982 THAT ADD UP TO THIRTY CENTS AND ONE OF THEM CANNOT BE A NICKEL.

Duh. The answer was a quarter and a nickel because the riddle said only *one* of them couldn't be a nickel.

So to win, Kyle had to find a 1982 quarter *and* a 1982 nickel.

Also easy.

Their dad kept an apple cider jug filled with loose change down in his basement workshop.

That's why Kyle and Mike were racing to get there first.

Mike bolted through the front door.

Kyle grinned.

He loved playing games against his big brothers. As the youngest, it was just about the only chance he ever got to beat them fair and square. Board games levelled the playing field. You needed a good roll of the dice, a lucky draw of the cards and some smarts, but if things went your way and you gave it your all, anyone could win.

Especially today, since Mike had blown his lead by choosing the standard route down to the basement. He'd go through the front door, tear to the back of the house, bound down the steps and then run to their dad's workshop.

Kyle, on the other hand, would take a shortcut.

He hopped over a couple of boxy shrubs and kicked open the low-to-the-ground casement window. He heard something crackle when his tennis shoe hit the windowpane, but he couldn't worry about it. He had to beat his big brother.

He crawled through the narrow opening, dropped to the floor, and scrabbled over to the workbench, where he found the jug, dumped out the coins, and started sifting through the sea of pennies, nickels, dimes and quarters.

Score!

Kyle quickly uncovered a 1982 nickel. He tucked it into his shirt pocket and sent pennies, nickels and dimes skidding across the floor as he concentrated on quarters. 2010. 2003. 1986.

"Come on, come on," he muttered.

The workshop door swung open.

"What the . . . ?" Mike was surprised to see that Kyle had beaten him to the coin jar.

Mike fell to his knees and started searching for his own

coins just as Kyle shouted, "Got it!" and plucked a 1982 quarter out of the pile.

"What about the nickel?" demanded Mike.

Kyle pulled it out of his shirt pocket.

"You went through the window?" said a voice from outside.

It was Curtis. Kneeling in the flower beds.

"Yeah," said Kyle.

"I was going to do that. The shortest distance between two points is a straight line."

"I can't believe you won!" moaned Mike, who wasn't used to losing *anything*.

"Well," said Kyle, standing up and strutting a little, "believe it, brother. Because now you two *losers* have to put all the junk back."

"I am *not* taking this back to Twinky!" said Curtis. He held up a very slimy, knotted rope.

"Oh, yes you are," said Kyle. "Because you *lost*. Oh sure, you *thought* about using the window . . ."

"Um, Kyle?" mumbled Curtis. "You might want to shut up . . ."

"What? C'mon, Curtis. Don't be such a sore loser. Just because I was the one who took the shortcut and kicked open the window and –"

"You did this, Kyle?"

A new face appeared in the window.

Their dad's.

"Heh, heh, heh," chuckled Mike behind Kyle.

"You broke the glass?" Their father sounded ticked off. "Well, guess who's going to pay to have this window replaced."

That's why Kyle Keeley had fifty cents deducted from his allowance for the rest of the year.

And got grounded for a week.

Halfway across town, Dr Yanina Zinchenko, the world-famous librarian, was walking briskly through the cavernous building that was only days away from its gala grand opening.

Alexandriaville's new public library had been under construction for five years. All work had been done with the utmost secrecy under the tightest possible security. One crew did the exterior renovations on what had once been the small Ohio city's most magnificent building, the Gold Leaf Bank. Other crews – carpenters, masons, electricians and plumbers – worked on the interior.

No single construction crew stayed on the job longer than six weeks.

No crew knew what any of the other crews had done (or would be doing).

And when all those crews were finished, several

super-secret covert crews (highly paid workers who would deny ever having been near the library, Alexandriaville, *or* the state of Ohio) stealthily applied the final touches.

Dr Zinchenko had supervised the construction project for her employer – a very eccentric (some would say loony) billionaire. Only she knew all the marvels and wonders the incredible new library would hold (and hide) within its walls.

Dr Zinchenko was a tall woman with blazing-red hair. She wore an expensive, custom-tailored business suit, jazzy high-heeled shoes, a Bluetooth earpiece and glasses with thick red frames.

Heels clicking on the marble floor, fingers tapping on the glass of her very advanced tablet computer, Dr Zinchenko strode past the control centre's red door, under an arch and into the breathtakingly large circular reading room beneath the library's three-story-tall rotunda.

The bank building, which provided the shell for the new library, had been built in 1931. With towering Corinthian columns, an arched entryway, lots of fancy trim and a mammoth shimmering gold dome, the building looked like it belonged next door to the triumphant memorials in Washington, D.C. – not on this small Ohio town's quaint streets.

Dr Zinchenko paused to stare up at the library's most stunning visual effect: the Wonder Dome. Ten wedge-shaped, high-definition video screens – as brilliant as those in Times Square – lined the underbelly of the dome like so many orange slices. Each screen could operate independently or as part of a spectacular whole. The Wonder Dome could become the constellations of the night sky; a flight through the clouds that made viewers below sense that the whole building had somehow lifted off the ground; or, in Dewey decimal mode, ten sections depicting vibrant and constantly changing images associated with each category in the library cataloguing system.

"I have the final numbers for the fourth sector of the Wonder Dome in Dewey mode," Dr Zinchenko said into her Bluetooth earpiece. "364 point 1092." She carefully over-enunciated each word to make certain the video artist knew what specific numbers should occasionally drift across the fourth wedge amid the swirling social-sciences montage featuring a floating judge's gavel, a tumbling teacher's apple and a gentle snowfall of holiday icons. "The numbers, however, should not appear until eleven a.m. Sunday. Is that clear?"

"Yes, Dr Zinchenko," replied the tinny voice in her ear.

Next Dr Zinchenko studied the holographic statues projected into black crepe-lined recesses cut into the massive stone piers that supported the arched windows from which the Wonder Dome rose.

"Why are Shakespeare and Dickens still here? They're not on the list for opening night."

"Sorry," replied the library's director of holographic imagery, who was also on the conference call. "I'll fix it."

9

"Thank you."

Exiting the rotunda, the librarian entered the Children's Room.

It was dim, with only a few work lights glowing, but Dr Zinchenko had memorized the layout of the miniature tables and was able to march, without bumping her shins, to the Story Corner for a final check on her recently installed geese.

The flock of six audio-animatronic goslings – fluffy robots with ping-pongish eyeballs (created for the new library by imagineers who used to work at Disney World) – stood perched atop an angled bookcase in the corner. Mother Goose, in her bonnet and granny glasses, was frozen in the centre.

"This is librarian One," said Dr Zinchenko, loud enough for the microphones hidden in the ceiling to pick up her voice. "Initiate story-time sequence."

The geese sprang to mechanical life.

"Nursery rhyme."

The geese honked out "Baa-Baa Black Sheep" in six-part harmony.

"Treasure Island?"

The birds yo-ho-ho'ed their way through "Fifteen Men on a Dead Man's Chest".

Dr Zinchenko clapped her hands. The rollicking geese stopped singing and swaying.

"One more," she said. Squinting, she saw a book sitting on a nearby table. *"Walter the Farting Dog."*

The six geese spun around and farted, their tail feathers flipping up in sync with the noisy blasts.

"Excellent. End story time."

The geese slumped back into their sleep mode. Dr Zinchenko made one more tick on her computer tablet. Her final punch list was growing shorter and shorter, which was a very good thing. The library's grand opening was set for Friday night. Dr Z and her army of associates had only a few days left to smooth out any kinks in the library's complex operating system.

Suddenly, Dr Zinchenko heard a low, rumbling growl.

Turning around, she was eyeball to icy-blue eyeball with a very rare white tiger.

Dr Zinchenko sighed and touched her Bluetooth earpiece.

"Ms G? This is Dr Z. What is our white Bengal tiger doing in the children's department? . . . I see. Apparently, there was a slight misunderstanding. We do not want him permanently positioned near *The Jungle Book*. Check the call number. 599 point 757 . . . Right. He should be in Zoology . . . Yes, please. Right away. Thank you, Ms G."

And like a vanishing mirage, the tiger disappeared.

3

Of course, even though he was grounded, Kyle Keeley still had to go to school.

"Mike, Curtis, Kyle, time to wake up!" his mother called from down in the kitchen.

Kyle plopped his feet on the floor, rubbed his eyes, and sleepily looked around his room.

The computer handed down from his brother Curtis was sitting on the desk that used to belong to his other brother, Mike. The rug on the floor, with its Cincinnati Reds logo, had also been Mike's when *he* was twelve years old. The books lined up in his bookcase had been lined up on Mike's and Curtis's shelves, except for the ones Kyle got each year for Christmas from his grandmother. He still hadn't read last year's addition.

Kyle wasn't big on books.

Unless they were the instruction manual or hint guide to a video game. He had a Sony PlayStation set up in the family room. It wasn't the high-def, Blu-ray PS3. It was the one Santa had brought Mike maybe four years earlier. (Mike kept the brand-new Blu-ray model locked up in his bedroom.)

But still, clunker that it was, the four-year-old gaming console in the family room worked.

Except this week.

Well, it *worked,* but Kyle's dad had taken away his TV and computer privileges, so unless he just wanted to hear the hard drive hum, there was really no point in firing up the PlayStation until the next Sunday, when his sentence ended.

"When you're grounded in this house," his father had said, "you're *grounded.*"

If Kyle needed a computer for homework during this last week of school, he could use his mom's, the one in the kitchen.

His mom had no games on her computer.

OK, she had Diner Dash, but that didn't really count.

Being grounded in the Keeley household meant you couldn't do anything except, as his dad put it, "think about what you did that caused you to be grounded."

Kyle knew what he had done: He'd broken a window.

But hey – I also beat my big brothers!

* * *

"Good morning, Kyle," his mom said when he hit the kitchen. She was sitting at her computer desk, sipping coffee and tapping keys. "Grab a Toaster Tart for breakfast."

Curtis and Mike were already in the kitchen, chowing down on the last of the good Toaster Tarts – the frosted cupcake swirls. They'd left Kyle the unfrosted brown sugar cinnamon. The ones that tasted like the box they came in.

"New library opens Friday, just in time for summer vacation," Kyle's mom mumbled, reading her computer screen. "Been twelve years since they tore down the old one. Listen to this, boys: Dr Yanina Zinchenko, the new public library's head librarian, promises that 'patrons will be surprised' by what they find inside."

"Really?" said Kyle, who always liked a good surprise. "I wonder what they'll have in there."

"Um, books maybe?" said Mike. "It's a *library*, Kyle."

"Still," said Curtis, "I can't wait to get my new library card!"

"Because you're a nerd," said Mike.

"I prefer the term 'geek'," said Curtis.

"Well, I gotta go," said Kyle, grabbing his backpack. "Don't want to miss the bus."

He hurried out the door. What Kyle really didn't want to miss were his friends. A lot of them had Sony PSPs and Nintendo 3DSs.

Loaded with lots and lots of games!

* * *

14

Kyle fist-bumped and knuckle-knocked his way up the bus aisle to his usual seat. Almost everybody wanted to say "Hey" to him, except, of course, Sierra Russell.

Like always, Sierra, who was also a seventh grader, was sitting in the back of the bus, her nose buried in a book – probably one of those about girls who lived in tiny homes on the prairie or something.

Ever since her parents divorced and her dad moved out of town, Sierra Russell had been incredibly quiet and spent all her free time reading.

"Nice shirt," said Akimi Hughes as Kyle slid into the seat beside her.

"Thanks. It used to be Mike's."

"Doesn't matter. It's still cool."

Akimi's mother was Asian, her dad Irish. She had very long jet-black hair, extremely blue eyes, and a ton of freckles.

"What're you playing?" Kyle asked, because Akimi was frantically working the controls on her PSP 3000.

"Squirrel Squad," said Akimi.

"One of Mr Lemoncello's best," said Kyle, who had the same game on his PlayStation.

The one he couldn't play with for a week.

"You need a hand?"

"Nah."

"Watch out for the beehives . . ."

"I know about the beehives, Kyle."

"I'm just saying . . ."

15

"Yes!"

"What?"

"I cleared level six! Finally."

"Awesome." Kyle did not mention that he was up to level twenty-seven. Akimi was his best friend. Friends don't gloat to friends.

"When I shot the squirrels at the falcons," said Akimi, "the pilots parachuted. If a squirrel bit the pilot in the butt, I got a fifty-point bonus."

Yes, in Mr Lemoncello's catapulting critters game, there were all sorts of wacky jokes. The falcons weren't birds; they were F-16 Falcon Fighter Jets. And the squirrels? They were nuts. Totally bonkers. With swirly whirlpool eyes. They flew through the air jabbering gibberish. They bit butts.

This was one of the main reasons why Kyle thought everything that came out of Mr Lemoncello's Imagination Factory – board games, puzzles, video games – was amazingly awesome. For Mr Lemoncello, a game just wasn't a game if it wasn't a little goofy around the edges.

"So, did you pick up the bonus code?" asked Kyle.

"Huh?"

"In the freeze-frame there."

Akimi studied the screen.

"Turn it over."

Akimi did.

"See that number tucked into the corner? Type that in the next time the home screen asks you for your password."

16

"Why? What happens?"

"You'll see."

Akimi slugged him in the arm. "What?"

"Well, don't be surprised if you start flinging *flaming* squirrels on level seven."

"Get. Out!"

"Try it. You'll see."

"I will. This afternoon. So, did you write your extra-credit essay?"

"Huh? What essay?"

"Um, the one that's due today. About the new public library?"

"Refresh my memory."

Akimi sighed. "Because the old library was torn down twelve years ago, the twelve twelve-year-olds who write the best essays on 'Why I'm Excited About the New Public Library' will get to go to the library lock-in this Friday night."

"Huh?"

"The winners will spend the night in the new library before anybody else even gets to see the place!"

"Is this like that movie *Night at the Museum*? Will the books come alive and chase people around and junk?"

"No. But there will probably be free movies, and food, and prizes, and *games*."

All of a sudden, Kyle was interested.

"So, exactly what kind of games are we talking about?"

"I don't know," said Akimi. "Fun book stuff, I guess."

"And do you think this new library will have equally new computers?"

"Definitely."

"Wi-Fi?"

"Probably."

Kyle nodded slowly. "And this all takes place Friday night?"

"Yep."

"Akimi, I think you just discovered a way for me to shorten my most recent groundation."

"Your what?"

"My game-deprived parental punishment."

Kyle figured being locked in a library with computers

18

on Friday night would be better than being stuck at home without any gaming gear at all.

"Can I borrow a pen and a sheet of paper?"

"What? You're going to write your essay now? On the bus?"

"Better late than never."

"They're due in registration, Kyle. First thing."

"Fine. I'll keep it brief."

Akimi shook her head and handed Kyle a notebook and a pen. The bus bounced over a speed bump into the school driveway.

He would need to make his essay really, really short.

He was hoping the twelve winners would be randomly pulled out of a hat or something and, like the lottery people always said in their TV commercials, you just had to "be in it to win it".

Meanwhile, in another part of town, Charles Chiltington was sitting in his father's library, working with the college student who'd been hired to help him polish up his extra-credit essay.

He was dressed in his typical school uniform: khaki slacks, blue blazer, button-down shirt and tastefully striped tie. He was the only student at Alexandriaville Middle School who dressed that way.

"What's a big word for 'library'?" Charles asked his tutor. "Teachers love big words."

19

" 'Book repository'."

"Bigger, please."

"Um, 'athenaeum'."

"Perfect! It's such a weird word, they'll have to look it up."

Charles made the change, saved the file, and sent the document off to the printer.

"Your dad sure reads a lot," said his ELA tutor, admiring the leather-bound books lining the walls of Mr Chiltington's home library.

"Knowledge is power," said Charles. "It's one of our fundamental family philosophies."

Another was *We eat losers for breakfast*.

Kyle and Akimi climbed off the bus and headed into the school.

"You know," said Akimi, "my dad told me the library people had like a bazillion different architects doing drawings and blueprints that they couldn't share with each other."

"How come?"

"To keep everything super secret. My dad and his firm did the front door and that was it."

The second they stepped into Mrs Cameron's classroom for homeroom period, Miguel Fernandez shouted, "Hey, Kyle! Check it out, bro." He held up a clear plastic binder maybe two inches thick. "I totally aced my essay, man!"

"The library dealio?"

"Yeah! I put in pictures and charts, plus a whole section about the Ancient Library of Alexandria, Egypt, since this is *Alexandria*ville, Ohio!"

"Cool," said Kyle.

Miguel Fernandez was super enthusiastic about everything. He was also president of the school's Library Aide Society. "Hey, Kyle – you know what they say about libraries?"

"Uh, not really."

"They have something for every chapter of your life!"

While Kyle groaned, the second bell rang.

"All right, everybody," said Mrs Dana Cameron, Kyle's registration teacher. "Time to turn in your extra-credit essays." She started walking up and down the rows of desks. "The judges will be meeting in the faculty lounge this morning to make the preliminary cut . . ."

Crap, thought Kyle. There were *judges.* This was not going to be a bingo-ball drawing like the lottery.

"Mr Keeley?" The teacher hovered over his desk. "Did you write an essay?"

"Yeah. Sort of."

"I'm sorry. I don't understand. Either you wrote an essay or you didn't."

Kyle halfheartedly handed her his hastily scribbled sheet of paper.

And unfortunately, Mrs Cameron read it. Out loud.

" 'Balloons. There might be balloons.' "

21

The classroom erupted with laughter.

Until Mrs Cameron did that tilt-down-her-glasses-and-glare-over-them thing she did to terrify everybody into total silence.

"This is your essay, Kyle?"

"Yes, ma'am. We were supposed to write why we're excited about the grand opening and, well, balloons are always my favourite part."

"I see," said Mrs Cameron. "You know, Kyle, your brother Curtis wrote excellent essays when he was in my class."

"Yes, Mrs Cameron," mumbled Kyle.

Mrs Cameron sighed contentedly. "Please give him my regards."

"Yes, ma'am."

Mrs Cameron moved on to the next desk. Miguel eagerly handed her his thick booklet.

"Very well done, Miguel."

"Thank you, Mrs Cameron!"

Kyle heard an odd noise out in the parking lot. A puttering, clunking, clanking sound.

"Oh, my," said Mrs Cameron, "I wonder if that's *him*!"

She hurried to the window and pulled up the blinds. All the kids in the classroom followed her.

And then they saw it.

Out in the visitor parking lot. A car that looked like a giant red boot on wheels. It had a strip of notched black boot sole for its bumper. Thick shoelaces crisscrossed their way up from the windshield to the top of a ten-foot-tall boot collar.

"It looks just like the red boot from that game," said Miguel. "Family Frenzy."

Kyle nodded. Family Frenzy was Mr Lemoncello's first and probably most famous game. The red boot was one of ten tokens you could pick to move around the board.

A tall, gangly man stepped out of the boot car.

"It's Mr Lemoncello!" gasped Kyle, his heart racing. "What's *he* doing here?"

"It was just announced," said Mrs Cameron. "This evening, Mr Luigi Lemoncello himself will be the final judge."

"Of what?"

"Your library essays."

5

Eating lunch in the cafeteria, Kyle stared at his wilted fish sticks, wishing he could pull a magic Take Another Turn card out of thin air.

"I blew it," he mumbled.

"Yep," Akimi agreed. "You basically did."

"Can you imagine how awesome that new library's gonna be if Mr Lemoncello and his Imagination Factory guys had anything to do with it?"

"Yes. I can. And I'm kind of hoping I get to see it, too. After all, I wrote a real essay, not one sentence about balloons."

"Thanks. Rub it in."

Akimi eased up a little. "Hey, Kyle – when you're playing a game like Sorry and you get bumped back three spaces, do you usually quit?"

"No. If I get bumped, I play harder because I know I

24

need to find a way to get back those three spaces *and* pull ahead of the pack."

"Hey, guys!" Miguel Fernandez carried his tray over to join Kyle and Akimi.

He was being followed by a kid with spiky hair and glasses the size of welders' goggles.

"You two know Andrew Peckleman, right?"

"Hey," said Kyle and Akimi.

"Hello."

"Andrew is one of my top library aides," said Miguel.

"Cool," said Akimi.

"Mrs Yunghans, the librarian, just confirmed that Mr Lemoncello is the top-secret benefactor who donated all the money to build the new public library. Five hundred million dollars!"

"She heard it on NPR," added Peckleman, who more or less talked through his nose. "So we did some primary source research on Mr Lemoncello and his connection to Alexandriaville."

"What'd you find out?" asked Kyle.

"First off," said Miguel, "he was born here."

"He had nine brothers and sisters," added Andrew.

"All of 'em crammed into a tiny apartment with only one bathroom over in Little Italy," said Miguel.

"And," said Peckleman, sounding like he wanted to one-up Miguel, "he *loved* the old public library down on Market Street. He used to go there when he was a kid and needed a quiet place to think and doodle his ideas."

"And get this," said Miguel eagerly. "Mrs Tobin, the librarian back then, took an interest in little Luigi, even though he was just, you know, a kid like us. She kept the library open late some nights and let him borrow junk from her desk or her handbag – thimbles and thumbtacks and glue bottles, even red Barbie doll boots – stuff he used for game pieces so he could map out his first ideas on a library table. Then . . ."

Andrew jumped in. "Then Mrs Tobin took Mr Lemoncello's sketch for Family Frenzy home to her husband, who ran a print shop. They signed some papers, created a company and within a couple of years they were all millionaires."

But Miguel had the last word: "Now, of course, Mr Lemoncello is a bazillionaire!"

"What are you four nerds so excited about?" said Haley Daley as she waltzed past with the gaggle of popular girls in her royal court. Haley was the princess of the seventh grade. Blond hair, blue eyes, blazingly bright smile. She looked like a walking toothpaste commercial.

"We're pumped about Mr Lemoncello!" said Miguel.

"And the new library!" said Andrew.

"And," said Kyle melodramatically, "just seeing you, Haley."

"You are *so* immature. Come on, girls." Haley and her friends flounced away to the "cool kids" table.

"Check it out," said Akimi, gesturing towards the

cafeteria's food queue, where Charles Chiltington was balancing two trays: his own and one for Mrs Cameron.

"I'm so glad you have lunchroom duty today, Mrs Cameron," Kyle heard Chiltington say. "If you don't mind, I have a few questions about how conventions within genres – such as poetry, drama or essays – can affect meaning."

"Well, Charles, I'd be happy to discuss that with you."

"Thank you, Mrs Cameron. And, may I say, that sweater certainly complements your eye colour."

"What a suck-up," mumbled Akimi. "Chiltington's trying to use his weaselly charm to make sure Mrs C sends his essay up the line to Mr Lemoncello."

"Don't worry," said Kyle. "Mrs Cameron isn't the final judge. Mr Lemoncello is. And since he's a genius, he will definitely pick the essays you guys all wrote."

"Undoubtedly," said Peckleman.

"Thanks, Kyle," said Miguel.

"I just wish you could win with us," said Akimi.

"Well, maybe I can. Like you said, this is just a Move Back Three Spaces card. A Take a Walk on the Boardwalk when someone else owns it. It's a chute in Chutes and Ladders. A detour to the Molasses Swamp in Candy Land!"

"Yo, Kyle," said Miguel. "Exactly how many board games have you played?"

"Enough to know that you don't ever quit until

somebody else actually wins." He picked up his lunch and headed for the dirty-tray window.

Akimi called after him. "Where are you going?"

"I have the rest of lunch and my free period to work on a new essay."

"But Mrs Cameron won't take it."

"Maybe. But I've got to roll the dice one more time. Maybe I'll get lucky."

"I hope so," said Akimi.

"Me too! See you guys on the bus!"

Working on his library essay like he'd never worked on any essay in his whole essay-writing life, Kyle crafted a killer thesis sentence that compared libraries to his favourite games.

"Using a library can make learning about anything (and everything) fun," he wrote. "When you're in a library, researching a topic, you're on a scavenger hunt, looking for clues and prizes in books instead of your attic or back-yard."

He put in points and sub-points.

He wrapped everything up with a tidy conclusion.

He even checked his spelling (twice).

But Akimi had been right.

"I'm sorry, Kyle," Mrs Cameron said when he handed her his new paper at the end of the day. "This is very good and I am impressed by your extra effort. However, the deadline was this morning. Rules are rules. The same as they are in all the board games you mentioned in your essay."

She'd basically handed Kyle a Go Back Five Hundred Spaces card.

But Kyle refused to give up.

He remembered how his mother had written to Mr Lemoncello's Imagination Factory when he and his brothers needed a fresh set of clue cards for the Indoor-Outdoor Scavenger Hunt.

Maybe he could send his essay directly to Mr Lemoncello via email.

Maybe, if the game maker wasn't judging the essays until later that night, Kyle still had a shot. A long shot, but, hey, sometimes the long ones were the only shots you got.

The second he hit home he sat down at his mother's kitchen computer. He attached his essay file to a "high priority" email addressed to Mr Lemoncello at the Imagination Factory.

"What are you doing, Kyle?" his mom asked when she came into the room and found him typing on her computer.

"Some extra-credit homework."

"Extra credit? School's out at the end of the week."

"So?"

"You're not playing my Diner Dash game, are you?"

"No, Mom. It's an essay. About Mr Lemoncello's amazing new library downtown."

"Oh. Sounds interesting. I heard on the radio that there's going to be a gala grand opening reception this Friday night at the Parker House Hotel, right across the street from the old bank building. I mean, the *new* library."

Kyle typed in a PS to his email: "I hope at the party on Friday you have balloons."

He hit send.

"Who did you send your essay to?" his mother asked. "Your teacher?"

"No. Mr Lemoncello himself. It took some digging, but I found his email address on his game company's website."

"Really? I'm impressed." His mom rubbed his hair. "You know, this morning, I said to your dad: 'Kyle can be just as smart as Curtis and just as focused as Mike – *when* he puts his mind to it.' "

Kyle smiled. "Thanks, Mom."

But his smile quickly disappeared when a *BONG!* alerted him to an incoming email.

From Mr Lemoncello.

It was an auto-response form letter.

Dear Lemoncello Game Lover:

This is a no-reply mailbox. Your message did not go through. Do not try to resend it or you'll just hear another *BONG!* But thank you for playing our games.

7

Heading back to school on Tuesday, Kyle knew he had to put on a brave face.

He smiled as he walked with his class towards the auditorium for a special early-morning assembly. The one where Mr Luigi L. Lemoncello himself would announce the winners of the Library Lock-In Essay Contest.

"I hope he picked yours," Kyle whispered to Akimi.

"Thanks. I do, too. But the lock-in won't be as much fun without you."

"Well, when it's over, and the library is officially open, you can take me on a tour."

"That's exactly what I'm going to do! *If* I win."

"If you don't, I'm sending a flaming squirrel after Mrs Cameron."

For this assembly, the seventh graders, most of whom were twelve years old, were told to sit in the front rows, close to the stage. That made Kyle feel a little better. At least he'd get a chance to see Mr Lemoncello up close and personal.

But his hero wasn't even onstage.

Just the principal; the school librarian, Mrs Yunghans; and a redheaded woman in high-heeled shoes who Kyle didn't recognize. She sat up straight, like someone had slipped a yardstick down the back of her bright red business suit. Her glasses were bright red, too.

"That's Dr Yanina Zinchenko!" gushed Miguel Fernandez, who was sitting on Kyle's right.

"Who's she?" asked Akimi, seated to Kyle's left.

"Just the most famous librarian in the whole wide world!"

"All right, boys and girls," said the principal at the podium. "Settle down. Quiet, please. It is my great honour to introduce the head librarian for the new Alexandriaville public library, Dr Yanina Zinchenko."

Everybody clapped. The tall lady in the red outfit strode to the microphone.

"Good morning."

Her voice was breathy with just a hint of a Russian accent.

"Twelve years ago, this town lost its one and only public library when it was torn down to make room for an elevated parking garage. Back then, many said the internet had rendered the 'old-fashioned' library obsolete, that a new parking garage would attract shoppers to the boutiques and dress shops near the old bank building. But the library's demolition also meant that those of you who are now twelve years old have lived your entire lives *without* a public library."

She looked down at the front rows.

"This is why, to kick off our summer reading programme, twelve twelve-year-olds will be selected to be the very first to explore the wonders awaiting inside Mr Lemoncello's extraordinary new library. You will, of course, need your parents' permission. We have slips for you to take home. You will also need a sleeping bag, a toothbrush and, if you please, a change of clothes."

She smiled mysteriously.

"You might consider packing *two* pairs of underwear."

OK, thought Kyle. *That's bizarre.* Did the librarian really think seventh graders weren't toilet trained?

"There will be movies, food, fun, games and prizes. Also, each of our twelve winners will receive a five-hundred-dollar gift card good towards the purchase of Lemoncello games and gizmos."

Oh, man. Five hundred bucks' worth of free games and gear? Kyle sank a little lower in his seat. The next time someone gave him an extra-credit essay assignment, he'd turn it in *early*!

"And now, here to announce our winners, the man behind the new library, the master gamester himself – Mr Luigi Lemoncello!"

Dr Zinchenko gestured to her left.

The whole auditorium swung their heads.

People were clapping and whistling and cheering.

But nobody came onstage.

The applause petered out.

And then, on the opposite side of the stage, Kyle heard a very peculiar sound.

It was a cross between a burp and the squeak from a squeeze toy.

8

Over on the side of the stage, a shoe that looked like a peeled-open banana appeared from behind a curtain.

When it landed, the shoe burp-squeaked.

As a second banana shoe burp-squeaked on to the floor, Kyle looked up and there he was – Mr Lemoncello! He had loose and floppy limbs and was dressed in a three-piece black suit with a bright red tie. His black broad-brimmed hat was cocked at a crooked angle atop his curly white hair. Kyle was so close he could see a sly twinkle sparkling in Mr Lemoncello's coal-black eyes.

Treading very carefully, Mr Lemoncello walked towards the podium. The burp-squeaks in his shoes seemed to change pitch depending on how hard he landed on his heels. He added a couple of little jig steps, a quick hop and a stutter-step skip, and yes – his shoes were squeaking out a song.

"Pop Goes the Weasel."

On the *Pop!* Mr Lemoncello popped behind the podium.

The crowd went wild.

Mr Lemoncello politely bowed and said, very softly, "Tank you. Tank you. *Grazie. Grazie.*"

He bent forward so his mouth was maybe an inch away from the microphone.

"*Buon giorno,* boise and-uh girls-a." He spoke very timidly, very slowly. "Tees ees how my-uh momma and my-uh poppa teach-uh me to speak-eh de English."

He wiggled his ears. Straightened his back.

"But then," he said in a crisp, clear voice, "I went to the Alexandriaville Public Library, where a wonderful librarian named Mrs Gail Tobin helped me learn how to speak like this: 'If two witches were watching two watches, which witch would watch which watch?' I can also speak while upside down and underwater, but not today because I just had this suit dry-cleaned and do *not* want to get it wet."

Mr Lemoncello bounced across the stage like a happy grasshopper.

"Now then, children, if I may call you that – which I must because I have not yet memorized all of your names, even though I *am* working on it – what do you think is the most amazingly incredible thing you'll find inside your wondrous new library, besides, of course, all the knowledge you need to do anything and everything you ever want or need to do?"

No one said anything. They were too mesmerized by Mr Lemoncello's rat-a-tat words.

"Would it be: A) robots silently whizzing their way through the library, restocking the shelves, B) the Electronic Learning Centre, with three dozen plasma-screen TVs all connected to flight simulators and educational video games, or C) the Wonder Dome? Lined with ten giant video screens, it can make the whole building feel like a rocket ship blasting off into outer space!"

"The game room!" someone shouted.

"The robots!"

"The video dome!"

Mr Lemoncello raced back to the podium and made a buzzing noise into the microphone.

"Sorry. The correct answer is – and not just because of Winn-Dixie – D) all of the above!"

The crowd went wild.

Mr Lemoncello whirled around to face his head librarian.

"Dr Zinchenko? Will you kindly help me pass out our first twelve library cards?"

It was time to announce the essay contest winners.

Dr Zinchenko placed a stack of twelve shiny cards on the podium in front of Mr Lemoncello.

"Please," he said, "as I call your name, come join me onstage. Miguel Fernandez."

"Yes!" Miguel jumped up out of his seat.

"Akimi Hughes."

"Whoo-hoo."

Kyle was thrilled to see his two friends be the first ones called to the stage.

"Andrew Peckleman, Bridgette Wadge, Sierra Russell, Yasmeen Smith-Snyder."

Yasmeen squealed when her name was called.

"Sean Keegan, Haley Daley, Rose Vermette and Kayla Corson."

Ten kids, all the same age as Kyle, were up onstage with his idol, Mr Lemoncello. He was not. Only two more chances.

As if reading his mind, Mr Lemoncello said, "Only two more," and tapped a pair of library cards on the podium. "Charles Chiltington."

"Gosh, really?" He dashed up to the podium and started pumping Mr Lemoncello's hand. "Thank you, sir. This is such an honour. Truly. I mean that."

"Thank you, Charles. May I have my hand back? I need it to flip over this final card."

"Of course, sir. But I cannot wait to spend the night in your library, or, as I like to call it, your athenaeum. Because, as I said in my essay, when you open a book, you open your mind!"

Finally, Charles the brownnoser let go of Mr Lemoncello's hand and went over to line up with the other winners.

"And last but not least," said Mr Lemoncello, "Kyle Keeley."

Kyle could not believe his ears. He thought he was dreaming.

But then Akimi started waving for him to come on up!

Dazed, Kyle made his way up the steps to join the others onstage. Mr Lemoncello handed Kyle a library card. His name and the number twelve were printed on the front. Two book covers – *I Love You, Stinky Face* and *The Napping House* – were on the back.

"Let's all pose for a picture, please," said the principal.

When everybody moved into position for the photographer, Kyle found himself standing *right next to* Mr Lemoncello.

He swallowed hard. "I'm a big fan, sir," he said, his voice kind of shaky.

"Why, thank you. And remind me – you are?"

"I'm Kyle, sir. Kyle Keeley."

"Ah, yes. The boy who proved what I've always known to be true: The game is never over till it's over. *BONG!*"

9

Kyle couldn't wait to tell his family the good news.

"I won the essay contest!" He showed them his shiny new library card.

"Congratulations!" said his mom.

"Way to go!" said his dad.

His brothers, Curtis and Mike, were more interested in Kyle's other card: his five-hundred-dollar Lemoncello gift card.

"It's good for twelve months," said Kyle.

"But you need to use it *now*," said Mike. "We need to go to the store tonight so you can buy me Mr Lemoncello's Kooky-Wacky Hockey."

"I can't."

"Why not?"

"I have to show my library card at the store to cash it in."

"And?"

"Um, I'm grounded, remember?"

"You know, Kyle," said his dad, looking at his mother, who nodded, "since you worked extra hard and did such a bang-up job on your essay, I think we might consider suspending your punishment."

"Really?"

"Really."

Kyle's mom and dad smiled at him.

The way they smiled whenever Mike won a football game or Curtis won the science fair.

After supper, all five Keeleys piled into the family van and headed off to the local toy store.

"Lemoncello's hockey game is awesome," said Mike as they drove to the store. "Especially when the penguins play the polar bears."

"I'm hoping to find a classic board game," mused Curtis. "Mr Lemoncello's Bewilderingly Baffling Bibliomania."

"Is that about the Bible?" asked their dad from behind the wheel.

"Not exactly," said Curtis, "although the Bible, especially a rare Gutenberg edition, may be one of the treasures you must find and collect, because the object of the game is to collect rare and valuable books by –"

"The penguins in Kooky-Wacky Hockey aren't from Pittsburgh like in the NHL," said Mike, cutting off Curtis.

"They're from Antarctica. And the polar bears? They're from Alaska."

Kyle had decided to divvy up his gift card five ways. To give everybody – including his mom and dad – one hundred dollars to play with.

As soon as they entered the toy store, the family split up, cruising the aisles with their own shopping carts. His mom was going to upgrade to Mr Lemoncello's Restaurant Rush. His dad was looking for one of Mr Lemoncello's complicated What If? historical games: What If the Romans Had Won the American Civil War?

Kyle hung with Curtis and Mike for a while. Being the one with the gift card made him feel like he was suddenly *their* big brother.

Mike quickly found his PlayStation hockey game and Curtis was in geek heaven when he finally found Bibliomania.

"They only have one left!" he gushed, tearing off the cellophane shrink-wrap and prying open the lid. He sat down right in the middle of the store and unfolded the board game on his lap. "You see, you start under the rotunda in this circular reading room. Then you go upstairs and enter each of these ten chambers, where you have to answer a question about a book . . ."

"Um, I think I hear Mom calling me," said Kyle. "She must need the gift card. Enjoy!"

And Kyle took off.

"*The store will close in fifteen minutes,*" announced a voice from the ceiling speakers.

Kyle flew up and down the aisles and grabbed a couple of board games he didn't own yet, including Mr Lemoncello's Absolutely Incredible Iron Horse—a game where you build your own transcontinental railroad, complete with locomotive game pieces that actually puff steam.

As Kyle was doing some quick math to see if he'd spent his one hundred dollars, Charles Chiltington rolled up the aisle with a cart crammed full with *five* hundred dollars' worth of loot. Games stacked on top of games were practically spilling over the sides. Mr Lemoncello's Phenomenal Picture Word Puzzler, one of Kyle's favourites, was teetering on the top.

"Hello, Keeley," said Chiltington with a smirk. He looked down at the three games sitting in the bottom of Kyle's shopping cart. "Just getting started?"

"No. I shared my gift card with my family."

"Really? Well, that was a mistake, wasn't it?"

Kyle was about to answer when Chiltington said, "So long. See you on Friday." Kyle wasn't 100 percent sure but Charles might've also muttered, "Loser."

Since the store was about to close, Kyle headed towards the checkout lanes. When he passed the customer service department, he saw Haley Daley.

"No," Kyle heard Haley say in a hushed tone to the clerk working the Returns window. "I do not want to return these items for *store credit*. I would prefer cash."

44

Kyle finally found his family, showed the cashier his library card, and paid for everything with a single swipe of his gift card.

"You know, Kyle," said his dad as the family walked across the parking lot, "your mother and I are extremely proud of you. Writing a good essay isn't easy."

"Maybe you'll be an author some day," added his mom. "Then you could write books that'll be on the shelves of the new library."

"Thanks, little brother," said Curtis, practically hugging his Bibliomania box.

"Yeah," said Mike. "This was awesome. Way to win one for the team!"

"Best 'family game night' ever," joked their dad.

Kyle was enjoying his rare moment of glory, playing Santa Claus for his whole family. As the week dragged on, Friday night and the library lock-in started to remind Kyle of Christmas, too: It felt like they would never come.

Then, finally, they did.

10

"Now this is what I call a party," said Kyle's mother as she helped herself to a bacon-wrapped shrimp from a tray being carried by a waiter in a tuxedo.

Kyle and his parents were in the crowded ballroom of the Parker House Hotel for the Lemoncello Library's Gala Grand Opening Reception. The Parker House was located right across the street from the old Gold Leaf Bank building and the cluster of office buildings, craft shops, clothing stores, and restaurants called Old Town.

"I'm going to see if I can find Akimi," Kyle said to his mom and dad.

"Give her our congratulations!" said his mom.

"We're proud of *her*, too," added his dad.

Kyle made his way through the glittering sea of dressed-up adults.

Even though his parents had put on fancy clothes for

the reception, Kyle was wearing "something comfortable to go exploring in", as instructed by the Lock-In Guide he'd received on Wednesday. He'd packed a sleeping bag and a small suitcase with a change of clothes, toiletries and yes, as requested, an extra pair of underpants.

Kyle saw Sierra Russell all alone in a corner near a clump of curtains. It didn't look like her mother had come to the party with her. Sierra, of course, had her nose buried in a book. Kyle shook his head. The girl was about to spend the night in a building filled with books and she was skipping all the free food and pop so she could read? That was just nutty.

Haley Daley, wearing a sparkly blouse, was posing for a wall of photographers who wanted to snap her picture. Her mother was at the party, too. While the cameras were focused on Haley's smile, Mrs Daley wrapped up a couple of chicken kebabs in a napkin and slipped them inside her handbag.

Now Kyle saw Charles Chiltington. Poor guy must not have read the memo about comfortable clothes. He was still wearing his khakis and blazer, just like his dad. Kyle figured the Chiltington family must own like three hundred pairs of pleated tan pants.

"Hey, Kyle!" Akimi waved at him from near a fake shrub curled to look like a Silly Straw.

"Hey," said Kyle.

"Did you remember to bring your library card?"

"Yep." Kyle pulled it out of his pocket.

"Huh," said Akimi. "I got different books on the back of mine. *One Fish Two Fish Red Fish Blue Fish* by Dr Seuss and *Nine Stories* by J. D. Salinger."

"Guess they're like baseball cards," said Kyle. "They're all different."

"Hey, you guys!" Miguel Fernandez, more excited than usual (which was saying something), pushed through the mob to join them. "Did you try these puffy cheesy things?"

"Nah," said Kyle. "I'm sticking to food I recognize."

"The 'puffy cheesy things' are called fromage tartlets," said Andrew Peckleman, coming over to join the group.

"Huh," said Kyle. "Good to know."

A waiter passed by with a tray loaded down with small boxes of Mr Lemoncello's Anagraham Cracker cookies.

"Oh, I love these," said Kyle, taking a box off the platter and opening it. "The cookies are in the shapes of letters. You have to see how many words you can spell."

"Cool," said Miguel, snagging a fistful of cookies out of Kyle's box. "Taste good, too!"

"Yep," said Kyle. "But the more you eat, the harder the game gets."

"Why?" asked Andrew Peckleman.

"Less letters," said Akimi, snatching two "B's" and a "Q" and wolfing them down. "Mmm. Barbecue-flavoured."

Kyle spread out the remaining cookies in his palm: U N F E H A V. He grinned as he deciphered an easy anagram. "HAVE FUN. Sweet."

"Ladies and gentlemen? Boys and girls?" Dr Zinchenko,

dressed in a bright red suit, strode to the centre of the ball-room. "May I have your attention, please? Mr Lemoncello will be arriving shortly to say a few brief words. After that, I will escort the twelve essay contest winners across the street to the library. Therefore, children, might I suggest that you eat up? Food and drink are not permitted any-where in the library except in the Book Nook Cafe, conve-niently located on the ground floor."

Miguel grabbed a few more puffy cheesy things.

When she thought no one was looking, Mrs Daley shoved a napkined bundle of bacon-wrapped shrimp into her handbag.

Akimi nibbled a couple of chocolate-dipped pretzel sticks.

"Aren't you gonna grab some more grub?" she said to Kyle.

"No thanks. I only like food I can play with."

"One last thing," announced Dr Zinchenko. "We, of course, want our winners to have fun tonight. However, I must insist that each of you respect my number one rule: Be gentle. With each other and, most especially, the library's books and exhibits. Can you do that for me?"

"Yes!" shouted all the winners except Charles Chil-tington. He said, "Indubitably."

"Good thing the library has dictionaries," muttered Akimi. "Half the time, it's the only way to figure out what Chiltington's saying."

Suddenly, all the adults in the ballroom started clapping.

Mr Lemoncello, looking like a beanpole wearing a tail-coat and a tiny birthday-party fireman's hat, strode into the room through a side door.

"Thank you, thank you," he said, stretching the elastic band to raise his kid-sized hat and tipping it towards the crowd. "You are too kind."

When he let go of the hat, it snapped back with a sharp *THWACK!*

"As Dr Zinchenko informed you, I'd like to say a few brief words. Here they are: 'short', 'memorandum', and 'underpants'. And let us pause to remember the immortal words of Dr Seuss: 'The more that you read, the more things you will know. The more that you learn, the more places you'll go.' Children? . . ."

Mr Lemoncello flourished his arm towards the ball-room doors.

"It's time to go across the street. Your amazingly spec-tacular new public library awaits!"

11

Eager to see what was inside the new library, the twelve essay contest winners quickly gathered behind Dr Zinchenko.

"This way, children," said the head librarian. "Follow me."

The crowd cheered as they marched out of the ball-room, all toting their sleeping bags and suitcases. There was more cheering (plus some hooting and hollering) when they reached the hotel lobby and went out the revolving doors into the street.

The new public library, with its glistening gold dome, took up half a downtown block, its back butting up against an old-fashioned office tower. The building was a boxy fortress, three storeys tall, with stately columns that acted like bookends, because the windowless walls had been painted to resemble a row of giant books lined up on a shelf.

"It's like a majestic Greek temple," gushed Miguel.

"And the world's biggest bookcase," added Sierra Russell, who had finally put away her paperback.

Velvet ropes lined a path across Main Street that led to a red carpet leading up a flight of steps to the arched entryway and seriously steel (not to mention *round*) front door.

Kyle had to smile when he saw what was tethered to the railings on either side of the steps: balloons!

A big bruiser – maybe six four, 250 pounds – in sunglasses and a black sports coat stood in front of the library's circular door, which had several large valve wheels like you'd see on a submarine hatch. The burly guard wore his hair in long, ropy dreadlocks.

"What's with that door?" asked Haley Daley, who, of course, had pushed her way to the front. "It looks like it came from a bank vault or something."

"It is the door from the old Gold Leaf Bank's walk-in vault," said Dr Zinchenko. "It weighs twenty tons."

Akimi turned around and whispered, "My dad designed the support structure for that thing. Check out the hinges."

Kyle nodded. He was impressed.

"Why a vault door?" asked Kayla Corson.

"Because," said Dr Zinchenko, "one sleepy Saturday, when Mr Lemoncello was your age, he was working in the old public library over on Market Street. He was so lost in his thoughts, he did not hear the sirens as police cars raced past the library to the bank, where a burglar alarm had just been activated. This door serves as a reminder to us all: our thoughts are safe when they are inside a library. Not even a bank robbery can disturb them."

Miguel was nodding like crazy. He could relate.

"It also helps us keep our most valuable treasures secure."

"There aren't any windows," observed Andrew Peckleman. "Probably to stop bank robbers from busting in. But shouldn't you people have added windows when you turned it into a library?"

"A library doesn't need windows, Andrew. We have books, which are windows into worlds we never even dreamed possible."

"An open book is an open mind," added Charles Chiltington. "That's what I always say."

Dr Zinchenko pulled out a bright red note card. "Before we enter, please listen very carefully. 'Your library cards are the keys to everything you will need,'" she read. "'The library staff are here to help you find whatever it is you are looking for.'"

She smiled slightly, tucked the card back into her pocket, turned to the security guard, and said, "Clarence? Will you do the honours?"

"With pleasure, Dr Z."

Clarence turned one giant wheel spun another and cranked a third.

Noiselessly, the twenty-ton door swung open.

*   *   *

53

The first thing Kyle could see inside was a trickling fountain in a grand foyer of brilliant white marble. The fountain featured a life-size statue of Mr Lemoncello standing on a lily pad in the middle of a shallow reflecting pool ten feet wide. His head was tilted back so water could spurt up from his mouth in an arc.

Kyle noticed a quote chiselled into the statue's pedestal: KNOWLEDGE NOT SHARED REMAINS UNKNOWN. – LUIGI L. LEMONCELLO

Beyond the fountain, through an arched walkway, was a huge room filled with desks.

When everybody had shuffled into the entrance hall, Dr Zinchenko turned to the security guard.

"Clarence?"

Clarence hauled the heavy steel door shut. Kyle heard the whir of spinning wheels, the clink of grinding gears, and a reverberating clunk.

"Wow!" said Miguel. "Talk about a lock-in!"

"I'll be in the control centre, Dr Z," said the security guard.

"Very well, Clarence."

Clarence disappeared behind a red door.

"Now then, children," said the librarian, "if you will all follow me into the Rotunda Reading Room."

As the rest of the group started filing into the gigantic circular room, Kyle checked out a display case beside the red door. A sign over it read "Staff Picks: Our Most

Memorable Reads." A dozen books were lined up on four shelves.

One cover in the middle of the bottom row caught Kyle's eye. It showed a football player wearing a number nineteen jersey dropping back to hurl a pass. Kyle made a mental note of the title: *In the Pocket: Johnny Unitas and Me.* Tomorrow morning, when the lock-in was over, he might use his library card to check it out for his big brother, Mike.

"Wow!"

Everybody gasped as they stepped into the Rotunda Reading Room and looked up. The entire underside of the dome looked like space as seen from the Hubble telescope: a dusty spiral nebula billowed up, a galaxy of stars twinkled and meteorites whizzed across the ceiling.

"Ooh!"

The space imagery on the ceiling dissolved into ten distinct panels, each one becoming a display of swirling graphics.

"Those are the ten categories of the Dewey decimal system," whispered Miguel, sounding awestruck. "See the panel with Cleopatra, the guy mountain climbing, and the Viking ship sailing across it? That's for 900 to 999. History and Geography."

"Cool," said Kyle.

Tucked beneath the ten screens in arched niches were incredible 3-D statues glowing a ghostly green.

"I believe those are holographic projections," said Andrew Peckleman, waving up at a statue that was waving down at him.

The room under the dome was huge. It was circular, with a round desk at the centre that was surrounded by four rings of reading desks.

Kyle saw that half of the rotunda was filled with floor-to-ceiling bookshelves. The other half had balconies on the first and second floors that reminded him of the open atrium of a hotel he and his family had stayed at once.

While everybody was gawking at the architecture, Dr Zinchenko said the words Kyle had been waiting to hear all day:

"Now then, who's ready for our first game?"

12

"Will everybody please line up behind that far desk in front of the Children's Room?" said Dr Zinchenko, gesturing towards one of the wooden tables in the outermost ring of the room.

"How many of you are familiar with Mr Lemoncello's classic board game Hurry to the Top of the Heap?"

Twelve hands shot up.

"Very good," said Dr Zinchenko.

Overhead, the Wonder Dome dissolved into a gigantic, curved Heap box top.

"This will be a live, three-dimensional version of that game. Each of you will be asked a trivia question. If you are able to answer it correctly, you will roll the dice and advance the equivalent number of desks. When you return to the starting point, you will move into the next concentric circle of desks. When you complete that ring, you will move into the next and so on. If one of you makes it all the way to my desk at the centre, you will be declared the winner."

"But we don't have any dice," said Yasmeen Smith-Snyder.

"Yes you do. See that smoky glass panel in the centre of the desk? It is actually a touch-screen computer, currently running Mr Lemoncello's dice-rolling app. Simply swipe and flick your fingers across the glass to toss and tumble the animated dice."

Dr Zinchenko placed a stack of red cards on her desk. She looked like the host of a TV game show. "Before we begin, are there any other questions?"

Charles Chiltington raised his hand.

"Yes, Mr Chiltington?"

"What will the winner win? After all, the prize is the most important part of any game."

Kyle didn't totally agree, but he was too excited about playing the game to say anything.

"Tonight's first prize," said Dr Zinchenko, "is this golden key granting the winner access to Mr Lemoncello's private and very posh bedroom suite up on the library's second floor. Instead of spending the night on the floor in a sleeping bag, you will be relaxing in luxury with a feather bed, a seventy-two-inch television screen and a state-of-the-art gaming console."

OK. Kyle was definitely interested in this particular prize.

Judging from the wide-open eyes and chorus of "oohs" and "wows" all around him, so was everybody else.

Dr Zinchenko flipped over the first question card.

"What major-league pitcher was the last to win at least thirty games in one season?"

Six players got it wrong before Kyle got it right.

"Denny McLain."

"Correct."

He swiped the glass panel, rolled a ten and advanced ten desks around the room.

"What United States Navy ship was once captured by the North Koreans?"

Miguel nailed that one: "The USS *Pueblo*." He flew twelve spaces around the room.

"What did *Apollo 8* accomplish that had never been done before?"

Akimi, Andrew Peckleman and Kayla Corson struck out on that one.

But Charles Chiltington knew the answer: "It was the first spacecraft to orbit the moon."

"Correct."

Chiltington rolled a five, landing him in last place.

Kyle's next question was tougher:

"Who was famous for saying, 'Book 'em, Danno'?"

"Um, that guy on *Hawaii Five-0*?"

"Please be more specific."

"Uh, the one with the shiny hair. Jack Lord?"

"That is correct."

Kyle breathed a sigh of relief. Thank goodness he and his dad sometimes watched reruns of old TV shows from the 1960s.

But when he flicked the computerized dice, his luck hit a brick wall. He rolled snake eyes and moved up two measly desks.

Meanwhile, Miguel went down with a question about Barbra Streisand. (Kyle wasn't exactly sure who she was.)

And Charles Chiltington surged ahead with a correct answer about the Beatles' "Hey Jude" and a double-sixes roll.

As the game went on, Kyle and Chiltington, the only players still standing, kept answering correctly and moving around the room, until they were both seated at a desk in the innermost ring – only six spaces away from Dr Zinchenko's desk and victory. Kyle was seriously glad he and his mom had played so many games of Trivial Pursuit – with the original, extremely *old* cards.

"Kyle, here is your next question: What song in the movie *Doctor Dolittle* won an Academy Award?"

Kyle squinted. He had that movie. An old VHS cassette tape that his mom had bought at a garage sale. Too bad they didn't have a VCR to watch it on. But even though he'd never seen the movie, he had read the front and back of the box a couple of times.

"Um, 'Talk to the Animals'?"

"Correct."

He started breathing again.

"Roll the dice, please, Mr Keeley."

Kyle did.

Another pair of ones. He moved up two spaces. Now he was only four desks away from winning.

"Mr Chiltington, here is your next question: Who was elected president in 1968?"

"I believe that was Richard Milhous Nixon."

"You are also correct."

Chiltington didn't wait for the librarian to tell him to roll the dice. He flicked his fingers across the glass pad.

"Yes! Double sixes. Again." He moved around the last ring of desks, tapping their tops, counting them off even though everybody knew his twelve was more than good enough to carry him to the finish line.

"Congratulations, Mr Chiltington," Dr Zinchenko said as she handed him the key to the private suite. "You are this evening's first winner."

"Thank you, Dr Zinchenko. I am truly and sincerely honoured."

"Congratulations, Charles," said Kyle. "Way to win."

"Get used to it, Keeley," he answered in a voice only the other kids could hear. "I'm a Chiltington. We never lose."

13

What happened next was extremely cool.

A holographic image of a second librarian appeared beside Dr Zinchenko at the centre desk. She looked a little like Princess Leia being beamed out of R2-D2 in *Star Wars*. Except she had an old-fashioned bubble-top hairdo, cat's-eye glasses and a tweed jacket with patches on the elbows.

"Here to present our official library lock-in rules," said Dr Zinchenko, "is Mrs Gail Tobin, head librarian of the Alexandriaville Public Library back in the 1960s, when Mr Lemoncello was your age."

Overhead, the Wonder Dome had shifted back to its ten Dewey decimal displays.

"How old is she?" asked Sean Keegan.

"She'd be a hundred and ten if she were still alive."

"But she's dead and working here?"

"Let's just say her spirit lives on in this hologram."

"Mrs Tobin's the one who helped Mr Lemoncello so much," Kyle whispered to Akimi. "When he was a kid."

"I know. Her hair looks like a beehive."

Kyle shrugged. "From what I've seen on TV, the 1960s were generally weird."

"Welcome, children, to the library of the future," said the flickering projection. "Dr Zinchenko will now pass out Lemoncello Library floor plans – your map and guide to all that this extraordinary building has to offer. Your new library cards will grant you access to all rooms except the master control centre – the red door you passed on your way in – and, of course, Mr Lemoncello's private suite on the second floor."

Charles Chiltington dangled his golden key in front of his face. "I believe you need *this* to enter that."

Mrs Tobin ignored him. She was a hologram. That made it easier.

"Security personnel are on duty twenty-four hours a day," she continued. "During your stay, all of your actions will be recorded by video cameras, as outlined in the consent agreements you and your parents signed earlier."

"Are we going to be on a reality TV show?" asked Haley, smiling up at a tiny camera with a blinking red light.

"It is a distinct possibility," said Dr Zinchenko.

"I like television," said the ghostly image of Mrs Tobin. "*Rowan and Martin's Laugh-In* is my favourite programme. Returning to the rules. The use of personal electronic devices is strictly prohibited at all times during the lock-in."

The security guard, Clarence, and a guy who looked like his identical twin brother entered the rotunda, each of them carrying an aluminum attaché case.

"Kindly deposit all cell phones, iPods and iPads in the receptacles provided by our security guards, Clarence and Clement. Your devices will be safely stored for the duration of your stay and will be returned to you at the conclusion of our activities. Also, you may use the desktop pad computers in this room to comb through our card catalogue and conduct internet research. However, these devices cannot send or receive email or text messages – whatever those might be. Remember, I retired in 1973. We still used carbon paper. And now Dr Zinchenko will walk you through the floor plan."

Everybody unfolded their map pamphlets.

"As you can see," said Dr Zinchenko, "fiction titles are located here in the reading room. The Children's Enrichment Room, with soundproof walls, is over there. Two fully equipped community meeting rooms as well as the Book Nook Cafe – behind those windows where the curtains are drawn – are also located on this floor. Upstairs on the first floor, you will find ten numbered doors, each leading into a chamber filled with books, information, and, well, *displays* related to its corresponding Dewey decimal category."

Kyle raised his hand.

"Yes?"

"Where's the Electronic Learning Centre?"

Dr Zinchenko grinned. "Upstairs on the second floor, where you will also find the Board Room, the Art and Artifacts Room, the IMAX theatre, the Lemoncello-abilia Room, the –"

"Can we go upstairs and play?" asked Bridgette Wadge. "I want to try out the space shuttle simulator."

"I want to learn how to drive a car!" said Sean Keegan. "A race car!"

"I want to conquer the world with Alexander the Great!" said Yasmeen Smith-Snyder.

Apparently, everybody was doing what Kyle had already done: checking out the "Available Educational Gameware" listed on the back of the floor plan.

"Early access to the Electronic Learning Centre will be tonight's second prize," said Dr Zinchenko. "To win it, you must use the library's resources to find dessert, which we have hidden somewhere in the building. Whoever does the research and locates the goodies first will also be the first one allowed into the Electronic Learning Centre. So use your wits and use your library. Go find dessert!"

Everybody raced around the room and sat down at separate desks to start tapping on the glass computer pads.

Well, everybody except Sierra Russell. She spent like two seconds swiping her fingers across a screen, wrote something down with a stubby pencil on a slip of paper, then wandered off to inspect the three-storey-tall curved bookcases lining the walls at the back half of the rotunda. Kyle watched as she stepped on to a slightly elevated platform with handles like you'd see on your grandmother's walker. It even had a basket attached to the front.

"Dr Zinchenko?"

"Yes, Ms Russell?"

"Is this safe? Because the book I want is all the way up at the top."

"Yes. Just make sure your feet are securely locked in."

Sierra wiggled her leg. Kyle heard a metallic snap.

"It's like a ski boot," said Sierra.

"That's right. Now use the keypad to tell the hover ladder the call number for the book you are interested in and hang on tight."

Sierra consulted the slip of paper and tapped some keys.

"The bottom of that platform you are standing on is a magnet," said Dr Zinchenko. "There are ribbons of electromagnetic material in the lining of the bookcases. The strength of those magnets will be modulated by our maglev computer based on the call number you input."

Two seconds later, Sierra Russell was floating in the air, drifting up and to the left. It was absolutely awesome.

"The hover ladder must use advanced magnetic levitation technology," said Miguel, seated at the desk to Kyle's right. "Just like the maglev bullet trains in Japan."

"Cool," mumbled Kyle.

And for the first time in his life, Kyle Keeley wanted to check out a library book more than anything in the world.

14

"How about we work together?" said Akimi when she sat down at Kyle's table.

"Hmmm?"

Kyle couldn't take his eyes off Sierra Russell. She had drifted up about twenty-five feet and was leaning against the railings of her floating platform, completely lost in a new book.

"Hello? Earth to Kyle? Do you want somebody else to get first dibs on the Electronic Learning Centre?"

"No."

"Then focus."

"OK. So how do we use our wits and the library to find dessert?"

Akimi nodded towards Miguel, whose fingers were dancing across the screen of his desktop's tablet computer.

"I think he's doing a search in the card catalogue," whispered Akimi.

"Why?"

"It's how you find stuff in a library, Kyle."

"I know that. But we're not looking for *books* about dessert. We need to find actual food."

Andrew Peckleman stood up from his desk and sprinted up a wrought-iron spiral staircase leading to the first floor. Two seconds later, Charles Chiltington was sprinting up the staircase behind him.

All the other players soon followed. Everybody was headed to the first floor and the Dewey decimal rooms. Miguel finally popped up from his desk and made a mad dash for the nearest staircase.

"It's got to be up in the six hundreds, you guys," he called out to Kyle and Akimi.

"Thanks," said Kyle. But he still didn't budge from his seat.

"I guess the six hundreds is the Dewey decimal category where you find books about desserts," said Akimi. "Maybe we should . . ."

"Wait a second," said Kyle.

"Um, Kyle, in case you haven't noticed, you, me and glider girl Sierra are the only ones still on this floor, and Sierra isn't really *on* the floor because she's floating."

"Hang on, Akimi. I have an idea." Kyle pulled out his floor plan. "Dessert is probably hiding in plain sight. Just like the bonus codes in Squirrel Squad. Follow me."

"Where to?"

"The Book Nook Cafe. The one room in the library where, according to what Dr Zinchenko told us back at the hotel, food and drinks are actually allowed."

They strolled into the cosy cafe.

"Whoo-hoo!" shouted Akimi.

The walls were decorated with shelves of cookbooks but several tables were loaded down with trays of cookies, cakes, ice cream and fruit!

"That's why the curtains were closed behind the windows into the rotunda," said Akimi. "So we couldn't see all this food. Way to go, Kyle."

Kyle did his best imitation of Charles Chiltington: "I'm a Keeley, Akimi. We never lose. Except, of course, when we don't win."

After everyone had dessert, Kyle and Akimi were the first ones allowed to enter the Electronic Learning Centre.

Kyle flew the space shuttle, making an excellent landing on Mars before crashing into one of Saturn's moons. Akimi rode a horse with Paul Revere. Then Kyle learned how to drive a stick-shift stock car on the Talladega racetrack while Akimi climbed into a tiny submarine to swim with sharks, dolphins and sea turtles – all of which were projected on the glass walls of her undersea simulator.

All the educational video games had 3-D visuals, digital surround sound and something new that Mr Lemoncello was developing for his video games: smell-a-vision. When you sacked Rome with the Visigoths, you could smell the smoky scent of the burning city as well as the barbarians' b.o.

After an hour, Dr Zinchenko ushered everybody else into the Electronic Learning Centre. They'd been watching George Washington debate George W. Bush (both were audio-animatronic dummies) in the "town square" at the centre of the 900s room.

At 10 p.m. they all tromped into the IMAX theatre, also on the second floor, to see a jukebox concert. 3-D images of the world's best musicians (living and dead) performed their hits "live." The best part was Mozart jamming with Metallica.

Finally, around three in the morning, Clarence and his twin brother, Clement, came to escort the kids to their sleeping quarters. The boys would roll out their sleeping bags in the Children's Room, just off the rotunda; the girls would be upstairs on the second floor in the Board Room. Charles Chiltington would be luxuriating all alone in Mr Lemoncello's private suite.

Exhausted from the excitement of the day – and crashing after eating way too much sugar – Kyle slept like a baby.

He only woke up because he heard music.

Loud, blaring music.

The theme song from that boxing movie *Rocky,* his brother Mike's favourite.

"Whazzat?" he mumbled, crawling out of his sleeping bag.

Kyle glanced at his watch. It was 11 a.m. He figured the library lock-in was officially over and this was the group's wake-up call.

The music kept blaring.

"This is how they wake up astronauts," groaned Miguel.

"Turn it off!" moaned Andrew Peckleman.

Kyle slipped on his jeans and sneakers and staggered out into the giant reading room.

"Dr Zinchenko?"

His voice echoed off the dome. No answer.

"Clarence? Clement?"

Nothing.

The *Rocky* music got louder.

Akimi leaned in from the second-floor balcony.

"What's going on down there?"

"I think they're trying to wake up astronauts," said Kyle. "On the moon."

He made his way to the front door and reached for the handle.

It wouldn't budge.

He jiggled it.

Nothing.

He jiggled harder.

Still nothing.

Kyle realized that the library lock-in might be over but they were still locked in the library.

15

"Everybody, please take your seats," Dr Zinchenko said to the parents gathered in a conference room at the Parker House Hotel.

"When do our kids come home?" asked one of the mothers.

"Rose has soccer at two," said another.

The librarian nodded. "Mr Lemoncello will –"

Just then, an accordion-panel door at the far end of the room flew open, revealing the eccentric billionaire dressed in a bright purple tracksuit and a plumed pirate hat. He was eating a slice of seven-layer birthday cake.

"Good morning or, as they're currently saying in Reykjavik, *gott síðdegi,* which means 'good afternoon', because there is a four-hour time difference between Ohio and Iceland, a fact I first learned spinning a globe in my local library."

Mr Lemoncello, his banana shoes burp-squeaking, stepped out of a room filled with dozens of black-and-white television monitors – the kind security guards watch at their workstations.

"Ladies and gentlemen, thank you for joining us on this grand and auspicious day. Today I am pleased to announce the most marvellously stupendous game ever created: Escape from Mr Lemoncello's Library! The entire library will be the board game. Your children will be the game pieces. The winner will become famous all over the world."

"How?" asked one of the fathers.

"By starring in all of my commercials this holiday season. TV. Radio. Print. Billboards. Cardboard cutouts in toy stores. His or her face will be everywhere."

Mrs Daley raised her hand. "Will they get paid?"

"Oh, yes. In fact, you'll probably want to call me The Giver."

"And what exactly does Haley have to do to win?"

"Escape! From the library. I thought the game's title more or less gave that bit away." Mr Lemoncello tapped a button in his pirate hat and an animated version of the library's floor plan was instantly displayed on the conference room's plasma-screen TVs.

"Whoever is the first to use what they find *in* the library to find their way *out* of the library will be crowned the winner. Now then, the children cannot use the front door or the fire exits or set off any alarms. They cannot go out the way they went in. They can only use their wits, cunning and intelligence to decipher clues and solve riddles that will eventually lead them to the location of the library's super-secret alternate exit. And, ladies and gentlemen, I assure you, such an alternate exit does indeed exist."

The parents around the table started buzzing with excitement.

"Participation, of course, will be purely optional and voluntary," said Mr Lemoncello, clasping his hands behind his back and stalking around the room.

Several parents pulled out cell phones.

"And please – do *not* attempt to phone, email, text, fax or send smoke signals to your children, encouraging them to enter the competition. We have blocked all communication into and out of the library. Only those who truly wish to stay and play shall stay and play. Anyone who chooses to leave the library will go home with lovely parting gifts and a souvenir pirate hat very similar to mine. They'll also be invited to my birthday party tomorrow afternoon." He held up his crumb-filled plate. "I've been sampling potential cake candidates for breakfast."

Mrs Keegan crossed her arms over her chest. "Will this game be dangerous?"

"No," said Mr Lemoncello. "Your children will be under constant video surveillance by security personnel in the library's control centre. Dr Zinchenko and I will also be monitoring their progress here in my private video-viewing suite. Should anything go wrong, we have paramedics, firefighters and a team of former Navy SEALs – each with the heart of a samurai – standing by to swoop in and rescue your children. It'll be like *The Hunger Games* but with lots of food and no bows or arrows."

"Why not just have the kids play one of your other games?" a parent suggested. "Why all this fuss?"

"Because, my dear friends, these twelve children have lived their entire lives without a public library. As a result, they have no idea how extraordinarily useful, helpful and funful – a word I recently invented – a library can be. This is their chance to discover that a library is more than a collection of dusty old books. It is a place to learn, explore and grow!"

"Mr Lemoncello, I think what you're doing is fantastic," said one of the mothers.

"Thank you," said Mr Lemoncello, bowing and clicking his heels (which made them *bruck* like a chicken).

"If any of you would like to check up on your children," announced Dr Zinchenko, "please join us in the adjoining room."

"Oh, they're a lot of fun to watch," said Mr Lemoncello. "However, Mr and Mrs Keeley, I'm afraid your son Kyle does not enjoy the theme song from *Rocky* quite as much as I do!"

16

Rocky had done its job.

Kyle – and everybody else locked inside the library – was definitely awake.

Even Charles Chiltington had come down to the Rotunda Reading Room from Mr Lemoncello's private suite. The only essay writer not with the group was Sierra Russell, who, Kyle figured, was off looking for another book to read.

"We're still locked in?" squealed Haley Daley.

"This is so lame," added Sean Keegan. "It's like eleven-thirty. I've got things to do. Places to be."

"Look, you guys," said Kyle, "they'll probably open the front door right after we eat or something."

"Well, where's that ridiculous librarian?" said Charles Chiltington, who was never very nice when there weren't any adults in the room.

"Yeah," said Rose Vermette. "I can't stay in here all day. I have a soccer game at two."

"And, dudes," said Sean Keegan, "*I* have a life."

"Do you children require assistance?" said a soft, motherly voice.

It was the semi-transparent holographic image of Mrs Tobin, the librarian from the 1960s. She was hovering a few inches off the ground in front of the centre desk.

"Yes," said Kayla Corson. "How do we get out of here?"

The librarian blinked, the way a secondhand calculator (the one your oldest brother dropped on the floor a billion times) does when it's figuring out a square root.

"I'm sorry," said the robotic librarian. "I have not been provided with the answer to that question."

"Will we be doing brunch here this morning?" Chiltington asked politely. "I'm not hungry, but some of my chums sure are. After all, it is eleven-thirty."

"The kitchen staff recently placed fresh food in the Book Nook Cafe."

"Thank you, Mrs Tobin," said Chiltington. "Would you like anything? A bowl of oatmeal, perhaps."

"No. Thank you, CHARLES. I am a hologram. I do not eat food."

"I guess that's how you stay so super skinny."

Kyle shook his head. The smarmy guy was oilier than a soggy sack of fries. He was even sucking up to a hologram.

Chiltington and the others traipsed off to have

breakfast, but Kyle and Akimi stayed with the holographic librarian.

"Um, I have a question," said Kyle.

"I'm listening."

"Is the library lock-in over? Are we supposed to go home now?"

"Mr Lemoncello will be addressing that issue shortly."

"OK. Thanks, Mrs Tobin."

"You are welcome, KYLE."

After the librarian faded to a flicker, Akimi said, "By the way, Kyle, before we leave, you need to check out that room I slept in last night."

"The Board Room?"

"Yeah. They call it that because, guess what? It's filled with board games!"

"All Lemoncellos?"

"Nuh-uh. Stuff from other companies. Some of it goes way back to the 1890s. I think it's Mr Lemoncello's personal collection. It's like a museum up there."

Kyle's eyes went wide. "You hungry?" he asked.

"Not really. We ate so much last night."

"You think we have time to check out this game museum?"

"Follow me."

The two friends bounded up a spiral staircase to the first floor, where they found another set of steps to take them up to the second.

When he entered the Board Room, Kyle was blown away. "Wow!"

The walls were lined with bookcases filled with antique games, tin toys and card games.

"This is incredible."

"I guess," said Akimi. "If, you know, you like games."

Kyle smiled. "Which, you know, I do."

They spent several quiet minutes wandering around the room, taking in all the wacky games that people used to play. There was one display case featuring eight games with amazingly illustrated box tops. A tiny spotlight illuminated each one.

"Wonder what's so special about these games," said Kyle.

"Maybe those were Mr Lemoncello's favourites when he was a kid."

"Maybe." But the slogan etched into the glass case confused Kyle: "Luigi Lemoncello: the first and last word in games."

"But these aren't Lemoncello games," he mumbled.

The first spotlighted game in the case was Howdy Doody's TV Game. After that came Hüsker Dü?, You Don't Say!, Like Minds, Fun City, Big 6 Sports Games, Get the Message, and Ruff and Reddy.

"It's a puzzle," Kyle said with a grin.

"I thought they were games."

"They are. But if you string together the first or last

word of each game title . . ." He tapped the glass in front of the first box on the bottom shelf. "You *get the message*."

"Really?" said Akimi, sounding extremely skeptical. "You're sure it's not just a bunch of junk somebody picked up for like fifty cents at a yard sale?"

"Positive." Kyle pointed to each box top as he cracked the code. "Howdy. Dü you like fun games? Get Reddy."

Miguel Fernandez barged into the Board Room.

"Here you are! We need you guys in the Electronic Learning Centre. Now."

"Why?"

"Charles Chiltington wolfed down his breakfast, then raced up here to finish the game he started last night so he can enter his name as the first high scorer."

"So?"

"The game he's playing is all about medieval castles and dungeons!"

This time Akimi said it: "So?"

"He's escaping through the sewers. The game has smell-a-vision. You ever smell a medieval sewer? Trust me, it is foul *and* disgusting."

The three of them dashed up the hall and entered the stinky room where Charles was sitting in a vibrating pedestal chair, thumbing his controller. As his avatar sloshed through a sewer pipe, the subwoofers built into his seat made every *SQUISH!* and *SPLAT!* rumble across the floor.

"Whoa!" said Kyle. "Knock it off, Charles. You're pumping out total tear gas."

"Because I'm in the sewers underneath the horse stables. It's the secret way out of the castle. I'm going to win another game. That's two for me, Keeley. How many for you?"

"Yo," said Miguel. "This room is two storeys above the cafe. The ductwork is connected."

"What's your point?"

"You're making everybody's food downstairs smell like horse manure!"

"Who cares? I'm winning."

Charles's chair went *FLUMP!* again.

But this time, Kyle smelled . . . pine trees?

Like one of those evergreen air fresheners people hang inside their cars.

"Aw, this stupid thing is broken." Charles jumped out of the chair and reared back to kick it.

"Um, I wouldn't do that if I were you," said Kyle.

"Why not?"

"Because there's a security camera over there and it's aimed right at you."

"What? Where?"

"See the blinking red light?"

Suddenly, an image of Kyle pointing up at the camera lens appeared on every video screen in the Electronic Learning Centre.

Until he was replaced by Mr Lemoncello.

17

"Excellent escape plan, Charles," said Mr Lemoncello on the video screens.

"Thank you, sir," said Chiltington, smoothing out his khaki pants. "And just so you know, I saw an ant crawling up the side of this seat. That's why I almost kicked it."

"How very thoughtful of you, Charles."

"Mr Lemoncello?" said Akimi.

"Yes?"

"How come the sewer started smelling like a pine tree?"

"Because I enjoy the odour of pine trees much more than the stench of horse poop. How about you?"

"Definitely."

"Now then, will everybody else please join us upstairs in the Electronic Learning Centre? I have a very important announcement to make."

Kyle heard feet clomping up the stairs and soon Andrew, Bridgette, Yasmeen, Sean, Haley, Rose and Kayla hurried into the room.

"Are we all here?" said Mr Lemoncello.

"Everybody except Sierra Russell," said Kyle.

"Ah, yes. I saw her downstairs reading *When You Reach Me* by Rebecca Stead. We'll reach her later. It's nearly noon and I'm eager to move on to the next round of our competition."

"What competition?" asked Yasmeen Smith-Snyder.

"The one we are about to begin."

"Sir?" said Sean Keegan. "I have stuff to do today."

"That's fine, Sean. You are, of course, free to leave. If any of the rest of you do not wish to stay and play, kindly deposit your library cards in the discard pile."

A tile in the floor popped open and an empty goldfish bowl atop an ornate column rose up about three feet.

"Just drop it in the bowl there, Sean. Attaboy. Follow the flashing red arrows in the floor to the nearest exit, where you will receive a lovely parting gift along with my everlasting admiration for your essay-writing abilities."

Bright red arrows danced across the floor. Sean followed them.

"What happens if we decide to stay?" asked Akimi.

"You will be given the chance to play a brand-new, exciting game!"

"Is there a prize for the winner?" demanded Haley Daley.

"Oh, yes."

Now Miguel shot up his hand. "Mr Lemoncello? What do we have to do to win?"

"Simple: Find your way *out* of the library using only what's *in* the library."

"Awesome!"

"Lame," mumbled Kayla Corson. "I'm outta here."

She plunked her library card into the fishbowl and followed the blinking arrows out the door.

"Does anyone else want or need to leave?"

"Sorry, sir. I have soccer at two," said Rose Vermette. "See you guys later." She dropped her card into the discard bowl.

The instant she did, bells rang, confetti fell from the ceiling, and every electronic console in the game room started *ding-ding-ding*ing.

"Congratulations, Rose!" cried Mr Lemoncello, who had put on a pointy party hat. "For sticking to your prior commitments, you will receive our special Prior Commitment Sticker prize: a complete set of Lemoncello Sticker Picture Games and a laptop computer to play them on! Enjoy."

Charles Chiltington stepped a little closer to the security camera as Rose Vermette skipped out of the room.

"Sir, might we assume that the prize for winning your brand-new game will be even better than a laptop computer?"

"Yes," said Mr Lemoncello, taking off his party hat. "You may so assume."

"I'm in," said Chiltington.

"Me too," said Kyle.

"Me too," added Akimi, Miguel, Andrew, Bridgette, Yasmeen and Haley.

Sierra Russell wandered into the room. Her nose was buried so deep in her book she didn't even notice Mr Lemoncello's gigantic face on all the video screens.

"Is something going on?" she said, mostly to her book pages.

"You bet!" boomed Mr Lemoncello.

Sierra's head snapped up.

"Oh. Hello, sir."

"Greetings, Sierra. Sorry to interrupt your reading. Just have a quick question: Will you be staying or leaving?"

"Well, sir, I'd like to stay. If that's OK?"

"OK? It is *wondermous*, another word I just made up. Now then, to read you the rules of the game – because every game needs rules – here is your friend and mine, Dr Yanina Zinchenko!"

The video screens switched to a close-up of the librarian with the red hair and glasses.

"Your exit from the library must be completed between noon today and noon tomorrow," said Dr Zinchenko.

Mr Lemoncello's head popped into a corner of her screen.

"Tomorrow's my birthday, by the way. Mark your calendars."

And he ducked back out of the frame.

"Our security guards will continue holding your cell phones," said Dr Zinchenko. "You may not use the library computers to contact anyone outside the building. You may, however, use them to conduct research.

"You may also request three different types of outside assistance: one 'Ask an Expert', one 'Librarian Consultation', and one 'Extreme Challenge'. Please be advised: The Extreme Challenges are, as the name implies, extremely difficult. If you pass the challenge, your reward will be great. However, if you fail, you will be eliminated from the competition."

Kyle figured he'd avoid asking for one of those – unless he extremely needed to.

"To use any of these 'lifelines,'" Dr Zinchenko continued, "simply summon Mrs Tobin."

Chiltington raised his hand.

"Yes, Charles?"

"Would you mind telling us what the prize will be for the winner?"

The video screen switched to an image of Mr Lemoncello, who had done some sort of quick change. Now he was wearing sunglasses and had a silk ascot tucked into his shirt collar. He looked like a flashy Hollywood movie star. From 1939.

"Fame and glory! The winner will become my new spokesperson and will star in all of my holiday promotions."

"We'll be famous?" gushed Yasmeen, fluffing up her hair and smiling at the security camera.

Haley stepped in front of Yasmeen. "I've done some modelling work. For Sherman's Shoes in Old Town."

Yasmeen stepped in front of Haley. "I was an extra in a hot dog commercial once . . ."

"Well, I'm a cheerleader; Yasmeen isn't . . ."

While the two girls continued primping and posing for the camera, Dr Zinchenko came back on-screen to quickly rattle off some final words.

"Your library cards are the keys to everything you will need. The library staff are here to help you find whatever it is you are looking for. The way out is not the way you came in. You may *not* use any of the fire exits. If you do, an alarm will sound and you will be immediately eliminated from the game. For safety purposes, you will be under constant video surveillance and you will be recorded. In the unlikely event of an emergency, you will be evacuated from the building. Creating an incident that requires evacuation will not count as having discovered a way to exit the library. Any questions?"

"Just one," said Andrew Peckleman, adjusting his goggle-sized glasses with his fingertip. "When exactly will the game begin?"

Mr Lemoncello's face reappeared on the screens.

"Good question, Andrew! Oh, my. It's noon! How about . . . let's say . . . oh, I don't know . . . *now*!"

18

The contestants raced down the stairs to the Rotunda Reading Room.

Kyle saw Haley Daley dash down another set of steps into the basement, to what the floor plan called the Stacks.

Miguel and Andrew, the two library experts, grabbed separate tables and started working the touch-screen computers. Bridgette Wadge did the same thing.

Charles Chiltington strolled out the arched doorway and into the foyer with the fountain.

Yasmeen Smith-Snyder was running around the circular room with her floor plan in front of her face, like someone frantically checking their text messages while racing down a crowded sidewalk.

Sierra Russell found a comfy chair and sat down.

To finish her book.

The girl definitely wasn't into the whole spirit of The Game.

"So, Kyle," said Akimi, "you want to form an alliance?"

"What do you mean?"

"It's what people do on reality shows like *Survivor*. We help each other until, you know, everybody else is eliminated and we have to stab each other in the back."

"Um, I don't remember hearing anything about 'eliminations.'"

"Oh. Right."

"But, hey, there was nothing in the rules that said we couldn't share the top prize. I just want to *win*!"

"Cool. So, we're a team?"

"Sure."

"Great," said Akimi. "I nominate you to be our captain. All in favour raise their hands."

Kyle and Akimi both raised their hands.

"It's unanimous," said Akimi. "OK. Let's go ask that antique librarian a question."

"What?"

"We both get to ask one question, right?"

"Right."

"OK, here's mine: 'Hey, lady – how do we get out of here?'"

"And you think she'll tell you?"

"No. Not really. So, what's your plan?"

"Well, I was thinking –"

Suddenly, Yasmeen shouted, "I win!"

The rest of them stopped whatever they were doing.

"It's just like last night when Kyle found dessert in the most obvious place. To get out of the library, all we have to do is use one of the fire exits. Duh."

She headed towards a hallway between the Book Nook Cafe and Community Meeting Room A.

Kyle stood up. "Um, Yasmeen? I think maybe you missed some of what . . ."

Charles Chiltington dashed into the room and shouted, "You're not going to win, Yasmeen. Not unless you beat me to that fire exit!"

He bolted towards the corridor.

Yasmeen bolted towards it, too.

"You guys?" said Kyle.

Kyle could see a red Exit light glowing at the far end of the hallway Charles and Yasmeen were sprinting down. Charles stumbled and fell. Yasmeen kept running. Harder. Faster. She slammed into the exit bar on the metal door.

Alarms sounded. Flashing red lights swirled. Somewhere, a tiger roared. Mr Lemoncello's voice rang out of the overhead speakers. "Sorry, Yasmeen. That's where your sidewalk ends. You broke the rules. You are out of the game. Your library card will be placed in the discard bowl and you will be going home."

As the fire exit door slowly swung shut and Yasmeen disappeared into the bright sunshine outside the library,

Kyle checked out Charles Chiltington, who would've been sent home if he hadn't stumbled and had reached the exit first.

The guy was smirking.

That was when it hit Kyle: Chiltington had faked Yasmeen out. He knew she couldn't win by going out a fire exit. But he ran down the hall to fool her into thinking she was doing the right thing.

Oh, yeah. Chiltington was definitely in it to win it.

No matter who he had to trample.

Whistling casually, Charles strolled back to the lobby.

"What's Chiltington doing out in the entrance hall?" said Akimi. "They told us the way out isn't the way in."

Before Kyle could answer, Andrew Peckleman started shouting at Miguel, who had wandered over to Peckleman's table.

"Get away! You're trying to steal my idea!"

"No, man," said Miguel. "I just happened to see your screen and I don't think that particular periodical –"

"You know what, Miguel? I don't really care what you think! This isn't school. This is the *public* library and you're not the boss in here, so just leave me alone!"

Miguel tossed up his hands. "No problem, bro. I was just trying to help."

"Ha! You mean help me lose." Andrew stormed up the closest spiral staircase to the first floor and the Dewey decimal rooms. Miguel, looking sort of sad, headed up a separate spiral staircase. Bridgette Wadge trailed after them.

"Want to follow those guys like Bridgette did?" whispered Akimi. "I'll take Peckleman, you take Miguel."

"No thanks," said Kyle, looking up at the domed ceiling. "I'm much more interested in the windows up there."

Three storeys above the rotunda floor, just below the Wonder Dome, there was a series of ten arched windows set between the recessed statue nooks. The windows acted like skylights at the base of the dome, allowing sunshine to flood into the room below.

"Do you think those windows open?" asked Akimi.

"Maybe. Maybe not. But I've never let a closed or locked window stand between me and winning a game. Just ask my dad."

"What?"

"Never mind. Come on." Kyle trotted over to the cushy chair where Sierra Russell was peacefully reading her book.

"Um, excuse me, hate to interrupt . . ."

Sierra raised her head. She had a very dreamy look in her eyes.

"I need a book."

"Really?" said Sierra. "What kind?"

"Like the one you found. Up there." He gestured to the curving bookcases climbing up the back half of the rotunda.

"Fiction," said Sierra.

"Right," said Kyle. "Love me some fiction."

"Well, what sort of story do you like?"

"Something way up high," said Kyle. "The higher the better."

"Really?"

"Yep."

"Well, that's an interesting way to put together a reading list, basing it on bookcase elevation . . ."

"I'd like something on the top shelf. Maybe right under the hologram statue of that guy hanging out with the Cat in the Hat."

"That's Dr Seuss," said Sierra. "He wrote *The Cat in the Hat*."

"Sweet," said Kyle. "But I just like how close he is to that window."

19

"Oh, Mrs Tobin?" Akimi called out. "I need to use my Librarian Consultation."

"You sure about this?" said Kyle.

"That's the beauty of being a team. After we burn through mine, we'll still have yours."

The hologram librarian appeared and advised Akimi that *Huckleberry Finn* by Mark Twain was the book located right underneath the holographic image of Dr Seuss and the Cat in the Hat.

After Mrs Tobin vanished, Kyle and Akimi used their desktop computer to find the call number for *Huckleberry Finn*. Kyle grabbed a pen and scribbled it down on his palm.

"Are you going to do what I think you're going to do?" said Akimi.

"Yep. I'm going to float up there, hoist myself into that nook where the hologram is, reach over to the window, push it open and stick out my hand. Technically, I will have found my way *out* of the library. Nothing in the rules said anything about how *far* outside we had to go to win."

"You could fall."

"I don't think so. I'm wiry, like a monkey."

"Seriously, Kyle. It isn't worth it."

"Um, yes it is. Did I mention I want to *win*?"

"You should improvise a safety harness," suggested Sierra Russell.

"Huh?"

"Well, in this adventure book I read once, the hero was in a very similar predicament. So he removed the curled handset wires from several telephones, bundled them together and made a safety rope."

Ten minutes later, Kyle, Akimi and Sierra had stripped the sproingy wires off a couple of telephone handsets. Kyle looped the cables around his waist and tied the other end to the handrail of the hover ladder. When fully extended, the safety rope would stretch out to a little more than twenty feet.

It should work.

"Be careful up there," said Akimi.

"Yes," said Sierra, who wasn't reading her book anymore. Apparently, watching a real live person risk his real live life by doing something really, really scary was one thing more exciting than reading.

Kyle locked his feet into the hover ladder's ski boot brackets. "Here we go."

Serious adrenaline raced through his body as he tapped the call number for *Huckleberry Finn* into the hover ladder's book locator keypad.

"When you open the window," said Akimi, "just shout, 'I found the way out!' and we win."

"Right," said Kyle. "All three of us."

"Huh?"

"Hey, Sierra came up with the safety rope idea. She's on our team now, too."

"Fine. Whatever. Just don't break your neck."

"Not part of the plan."

Kyle pressed the enter button on the control panel. The platform floated up off the ground and drifted slightly to the right.

"Be careful!" said Akimi. "Watch it!"

"I'm not doing anything," said Kyle. "This thingama-jiggy is doing all the work. I'm just along for the ride."

Kyle gripped the handles as the platform rose higher and higher. He sailed past books by Tolstoy and Thackeray. Tilting back his head, he looked up at the semi-transparent statues projected into the curved niches next to the arched windows.

They were a weird mix. A thoughtful African American man in a three-piece suit and a bow tie. A guy with long curly hair, old-fashioned clothes and a looking glass. A long-haired dude in a scruffy shirt hiding behind cutouts of the letters "P" and "B". A bald guy with a beard.

Since the statues were really holographic projections, they had chisel-type labels floating in front of their pedestals identifying who the famous people were. The ones closest to Kyle were George Orwell, Lewis Carroll, Dr Seuss and Maya Angelou.

As he continued to climb, Kyle could hear the soft whir of the electromagnets invisibly lifting him towards the ceiling.

And then he heard something much louder.

"What a ridiculous idea!"

Charles Chiltington. He was standing on the first-floor balcony at the far side of the rotunda.

"You know, Keeley, I thought about doing the same thing. But then I noticed something you obviously overlooked: There's a wire mesh security screen on the other side of those windows."

The levitating platform stuttered to a stop.

"Enjoy staring at the ceiling, Keeley. I'm off to win yet another game!"

Kyle ignored Chiltington and grabbed hold of the ledge beneath Dr Seuss's berth. He tried to haul himself up but his feet wouldn't budge.

They were locked in place by those ski boot clamps.

And this close to the skylights, Kyle could see that Chiltington was right – there was a security screen on the other side of the windows.

Kyle checked his wristwatch. It was 1 p.m. He and

his teammates had wasted an hour on the lame window idea. He sighed heavily and stared up at the quivering Seuss projection in the bowed niche above his head.

The Cat in the Hat's mouth started to move.

" 'Think left and think right and think low and think high.' "

Kyle recognized the voice.

It was Mr Lemoncello.

" 'Oh, the thinks you can think up if only you try!' "

In other words, Kyle was back to square one. He needed to think up a whole new escape plan.

The ladder began a slow and steady descent to the floor – even though Kyle hadn't pushed a button.

"Don't listen to smarmypants Charles," Akimi coached as Kyle coasted towards the floor. "It was worth a shot."

"I agree," said Sierra.

A bloodcurdling scream came ringing up the staircase from the basement.

"That's Haley!" said Akimi. "I saw her go downstairs."

"That's where the Stacks are," added Sierra.

"Come on," said Kyle. "She could be in serious trouble."

"You should never help your competition, Keeley," scoffed Charles as he casually strolled down a spiral staircase. "Unless, of course, you *always* play to lose!"

20

Losers.

That's what Charles Chiltington thought about sentimental saps like Kyle Keeley. A damsel in distress starts screaming and he forgets all about winning the game to go rescue her?

What a pathetic loser.

Unless, of course, Haley Daley was screaming because she had already found the alternate exit.

That made Charles laugh.

Impossible.

Although quite pretty, Haley Daley, the princess of the seventh grade, was a total airhead. There was no way a dumb girl like her could've outsmarted Charles Chiltington.

It was time to play his hunch.

Twice already, the head librarian, Dr Zinchenko, had said, "The library staff is here to help you find whatever it is you are looking for." She said it once when they were just about to enter the library, again when she was reading the laundry list of rules.

Well, what Charles was looking for was a way out of the building that wasn't the front door and wouldn't set off any alarms.

That was why he kept coming back to the lobby with the gurgling fountain. Why he kept studying the display case labelled "Staff Picks: Our Most Memorable Reads".

"The staff are here to help," he muttered. "These are staff picks. Ipso facto, this has to be some sort of enormous clue."

Inside the sealed bookcase, Charles saw twelve book covers.

One for each of the twelve twelve-year-old players? he wondered.

The display items weren't actual books. They were cover art mounted on book-sized foam core. Three covers were lined up on each of the case's four shelves. Since they weren't actual books with spines, none of the covers included their call numbers.

Charles focused on the three books lined up on the bottom row.

Hoosier Hospitality was on the left. *In the Pocket: Johnny Unitas and Me* was in the middle. *The Dinner Party* was on the right.

Charles decided to concentrate on the Johnny Unitas

title. He moved into the rotunda and did a quick card catalogue search on one of the desktop computers. When he typed *"In the Pocket"*, a matching cover image popped up.

But still no call number.

In the spot where the identifier should have been, there were instead a censor's thick black box and the words "ID Temporarily Removed from System."

Scrolling further down the screen, Charles came across a rather unusual annotation: "You didn't really think we'd make it that easy, did you?"

Charles grinned.

The computer was telling him he was on the right track.

He glanced up from the desk. The Children's Room was directly in front of him. The book about Johnny Unitas, with its cartoony cover depicting a football player wearing a number nineteen jersey and dropping back to launch a pass, was most likely a children's book.

Of course, it was also a sports biography.

So would it be shelved with sports books, biographies or children's books?

Charles went back to the computerized card catalogue. He read the book's description: "Billy wants to be a great quarterback like his hero, Johnny Unitas, but his coach is worried he'll get hurt."

It sounded like fiction. A made-up story. It had to be in the Children's Room.

As Charles crossed the slick marble floor, something else struck him.

This was like Hüsker Dü?, a memory game he had played when he was in kindergarten. He was on a hunt to find a hidden match for the football book cover he had just memorized. This was, in short, another memory game – that was why the Staff Picks display had been subtitled "Our Most *Memorable* Reads."

"Clever, Lemoncello," he mumbled. "Very clever indeed."

Charles entered the children's department. It didn't take him very long to find the book, because *In the Pocket* was propped up on a miniature stand on top of a shelf.

"Found it!" Charles proclaimed. Then, savouring the moment, he picked up the book and read the title out loud: *"In the Pocket: Johnny Unitas and Me."*

All of a sudden, a row of animatronic geese tucked into a corner of the room started honking and singing.

"They call him Mr Touchdown, yes, they call him Mr T."

The squawking birds startled Charles so much he dropped the book.

When he did, a four-by-four card fluttered out from behind its cover.

Charles bent down to pick it up.

Printed on the card was a black-and-white silhouette. A quarterback, wearing a number nineteen jersey (just like Johnny Unitas), was arching back his arm to throw a pass.

19

Charles grinned.

He was definitely on the right track.

He tucked the silhouette card into his pocket and hurried back to the lobby to memorize more book covers.

21

"Ouch! I'm stuck! Help!"

Haley Daley's cries sailed up the staircase as Kyle led the charge down the steps into the Stacks.

"So, what exactly are the Stacks?" asked Akimi, three steps behind Kyle.

"It's where the library stores its collection of research material," said Sierra, who was two stairs behind Akimi.

The three of them reached the basement. It was filled with tidy rows of floor-to-ceiling shelving units.

"Help!"

Haley sounded like she was on the far side of the room, behind the walls of metal storage racks crowded with boxes, books, and bins.

"What is all this stuff?" said Kyle, looking for a passageway, trying to figure out how to get to wherever Haley was.

"Mostly rare books and documents you can't check out," said Sierra. "But if you fill out a call slip, you can use this material up in the reading room."

With a whir and whoosh of its electric motor, a shiny robot the colour of the storm troopers in *Star Wars* scooted across an intersection between bookshelves. It moved on tank treads and had what looked like a shopping cart attached to its front.

"Let's follow that robot!" said Kyle. "It might know the fastest way to reach Haley."

The trio dashed up a narrow pathway to where they saw the robot extending its quadruple-jointed mechanical arm to pluck a flat metal box out of a slide-in compartment. The box had been stored in a section of shelving with a flashing LCD that read "Magazines & Periodicals. 1930s."

"Somebody upstairs wants an old magazine?" said Akimi.

"They're probably researching the Gold Leaf Bank building," said Sierra. "I think it was built in the 1930s."

"Help!" screamed Haley. "I'm stuck."

"Hang on!" shouted Kyle. "We're coming."

"Well, hurry up already!"

"This way," said Kyle.

They scampered up another aisle, turned right and saw Haley, her hand jammed through a horizontal slot near the top of the basement wall. To reach it, she'd had to stand on an elevated treadmill maybe thirty feet long. Since the thing was rolling, Haley was jogging in place so she wouldn't fall on her face. The high-tech conveyor belt was actually a series of rollers. Ten robot carts – staggered so no two were directly across from each other – were lined up on either side.

"I think it's an automatic book sorter," said Sierra. "That laser beam near Haley's ankles probably scans a book's tag and tells the conveyor belt which of the ten sorting trays to shove it into."

"You guys?" screamed Haley. "Hurry up and rescue me!"

Kyle stepped back. Tried to assess the situation.

"What is that slot you're hanging on to?"

"The bottom of the stupid book drop," said Haley, trotting on the treadmill. "I saw it on the floor plan. People can walk up to it on the sidewalk and return their books. I figured it had to lead down here."

"Smart move," said Kyle. "You could crawl through the slot and escape."

"*If* you were the size of a book," Akimi said sarcastically.

"I never got that far," said Haley. "The minute I stepped on to this belt thing, it started moving."

Kyle nodded. "Probably a weight-activated switch."

"A book falls in," said Akimi. "The sorter starts up."

"Clever," said Kyle. "Plus, it gives our game its first booby trap."

"Well, the game is no fun if you're the booby stuck in the trap!" said Haley.

Kyle turned to Sierra. "We need to stop the belt so Haley can yank her hand out of that slot without falling on her butt or cracking open her skull. Have you ever read a book where the hero outwits an escalator or a rolling checkout belt in the grocery store or something?"

"No," said Sierra. "Not really."

"How about one where the hero just flips an emergency shutoff switch?" asked Akimi. "Because that's what I'd do if, you know, I found one."

Akimi was standing next to a wall-mounted switch box. She flicked it down. The conveyor belt slowed to a stop.

"Ta-da! Another chapter for my amazingly awesome autobiography – if I ever write one."

Haley yanked her hand out of the book return slot. It sort of popped when it finally sprang free. She collapsed to her knees on the frozen treadmill.

"My hand feels flatter than a pancake," she moaned.

"Are you hurt?" asked Kyle. "Maybe we should tell the security guys that . . ."

"What? That I have a boo-boo and need to go home? Forget it, Kyle Keeley. You're not going to beat me that easily."

"I'm not trying to –"

Haley showed him the palm of her hand. "Save it, Keeley." She crawled off the conveyor belt. "One way or another, I'm going to win this game. I just hope starring in Mr Lemoncello's commercials earns me some decent money."

She hobbled around the bookshelves towards the staircase up to the reading room.

When she was gone, Akimi raised her hand. "Question?"

"Yeah?" said Kyle.

"How come the guys inside the control room didn't flip a switch to shut down the book sorter when they saw Haley doing her cardio cha-cha-cha on it?"

Kyle shrugged. "Maybe they weren't watching."

"Actually," said Sierra, pointing to a square tile on the floor near the book sorter, "I think they were."

Kyle looked down. The tile was glowing like one of the tablet computer screens upstairs in the rotunda. Kyle read the words zipping across the illuminated square.

"'Congratulations,'" he read out loud. "'For helping Haley and being a sport, you've earned much more than a good report.'"

The tile popped open.

Inside a small compartment was a rolled-up tube of paper with a yellow card clipped to its end.

"Huh," said Akimi. "I guess somebody *was* watching."

Kyle pulled the yellow card off the paper tube. It smelled like lemons.

"What's it say?" asked Sierra.

Kyle flipped the card over so Sierra and Akimi could see what was printed on it:

SUPER-DOOPER BONUS CLUE.

22

"Oh, man, that was so dumb!"

Haley could not believe how idiotic she had been.

"Trying to crawl out of a book return slot? Chya. Like that was going to work."

She was giving herself a good talking-to as she trudged up the steps to the ground floor.

When she entered the rotunda, she saw Charles Chiltington slipping out into the lobby again.

Chiltington was a snake. Worse. A garden slug. Maybe a leech. Something oily and slimy that left a greasy trail and liked to mooch off other people's ideas. That was why Chiltington had tailed the twin library nerds, Peckleman and Fernandez, upstairs during last night's dessert hunt. Haley was smart enough to know that Chiltington was hoping to steal the book geeks' ideas.

Actually, Haley was a lot smarter than anybody (except

her teachers and whoever scored her IQ tests) knew. With certain people, mainly grown-ups and silly boys, pretending to be a ditzy princess made getting what she wanted a whole lot easier.

And what she wanted right now was money. Lots of money. Her dad had been out of work for nearly a year. They'd run through all their rainy-day savings. They'd had to borrow from relatives and in-laws.

If Haley could win this competition and become Mr Lemoncello's spokesmodel, her family's money woes would be over and they wouldn't have to sell their home. And once other people saw her on TV for Lemoncello games, they'd want her for their commercials, too. And movies. Maybe her own sitcom. Something on the Disney Channel.

But for all that to happen, Haley needed a winning idea – and fast. Something better than "crawl through a slot that's barely wide enough for your wrist." Maybe she should flush herself down the toilet and escape through the sewers like Charles did in that video game.

She headed over to the Book Nook Cafe so she could sit down and think.

She stepped into the room and checked out the snack table. There were trays of cookies, strawberries, bananas and brownies. Sitting down to nibble on a macaroon, she studied the row of cookbooks displayed on the bookshelves lining the wall.

One in particular caught her eye: *Cupcakes, Cookies & Pie, Oh, My!*

Because the cover looked extremely familiar: two googly-eyed sheep made out of chocolate-frosted cakes with gobs of mini marshmallows for fleece. Haley had seen the cover before.

In the lobby!

It was in that glass case of memorable reads selected by the library staff.

She went over to the shelf and picked up the book. When she opened the cover, she discovered two cards.

One was a four-by-four piece of white cardboard with the black silhouette of a sheep on it.

The second card was yellow and about the same size as a Community Chest card in Monopoly. Haley sniffed the card. It smelled like lemons.

She grinned. "For *Lemon*cello!"

On one side of the yellow card was printed:

SUPER-DOOPER BONUS CLUE

On the other was the clue:

YOUR MARVELLOUS MEMORY HAS EARNED YOU EVEN MORE MEMORIES. PROCEED TO THE LEMONCELLO-ABILIA ROOM.

LOOK FOR ITEM #12.

Haley slid both cards into the back pocket of her jeans,

pulled out her library floor plan, and found the Lemoncello-abilia Room. It was up on the second floor.

Making certain nobody (i.e., Charles Chiltington) was following her, Haley quietly dashed up a spiral staircase to the first floor. Checking for Chiltington one more time, she tiptoed up to the second floor, where she found the room labelled "Lemoncello-abilia: Mini-Museum of Personally Interesting and Somewhat Quirky Junk".

Haley opened the door and stepped inside.

The front room was like a storage warehouse. Cardboard boxes were stacked on top of wooden crates sitting on plastic bins stuffed with papers. All the boxes, bins and crates were numbered. She saw one labelled "#576".

"Guess Mr Lemoncello never throws anything away," Haley remarked as she scanned the heaps, looking for the #12 mentioned on her bonus card.

Weaving her way through the stacks and columns, Haley finally found her Super-Dooper Bonus. Item #12 was an old boot box from an Alexandriaville shoe store Haley had never heard of. Someone had taped a label on the lid: "Paraphernalia, Accoutrements and Doodads from Mr Lemoncello's 12th Year."

Haley lifted the lid. The box was filled with all sorts of confusing knickknacks: hand-whittled prototypes for game pieces; a star-spangled, red-white-and-blue "H-H-H Humphrey" button; a battered clasp envelope sealed up with tons of tape.

Someone had scribbled "First and Worst Idea Ever" on the front of the envelope with a Magic Marker.

There were also a felt flag from Disneyland and a rubber-banded stack of cartoony cards for something called Wacky Packages. (The card on top was Weakies, Breakfast of Chumps.)

Haley knew this memory box had to be an important clue.

Why? She had absolutely no idea.

23

Kyle flipped over his lemon-scented Super-Dooper Bonus card and read what was written on the other side.

YOU WILL FIND THE ULTIMATE VERSION OF THIS BOARD GAME ON THE FIRST-FLOOR BALCONY CIRCLING THE ROTUNDA.

"Huh?" said Akimi. "What's that mean?"

"I don't know. Let's roll out the paper and see."

Akimi and Sierra helped Kyle anchor the edges of the scroll on the tiled floor.

"OK," said Kyle. "It looks like the early sketch for a board game. See the circle in the centre of the other circle? That's probably where you place the spinner. You move your pieces around the ten rooms . . ."

He stopped.

"Wait a second."

"What?" said Akimi.

"Do you recognize the game?" asked Sierra.

"Yep," said Kyle. "I played it this week with my brother Curtis. It's Mr Lemoncello's Bewilderingly Baffling Bibliomania. It takes place in a make-believe *library*."

"What about finding the 'ultimate version' up on the first-floor balcony?" asked Sierra.

Kyle grinned. "You'll see."

Coming up from the basement, Kyle saw Andrew Peckleman in the middle of the Rotunda Reading Room, opening a long metal box sitting on top of the centre desk.

The holographic image of Mrs Tobin was there, smiling patiently, as Peckleman pulled some kind of magazine out of the box. Miguel was also near the librarian's desk, apparently waiting his turn for a consultation.

"That's the box we saw the robot pluck off the shelf," whispered Akimi.

Kyle nodded. He motioned for the others to follow him and slipped around the circumference of the rotunda. Akimi and Sierra slunk after him.

In the shadows on the far side of the room, they saw Haley Daley heading for the staircase they'd just come up: steps that would take her back to the basement.

Kyle wondered if she'd found something else to crawl through. If so, he hoped it was bigger than a mailbox.

"Is this the *real* magazine?" he heard Peckleman shout at the hologram.

"Yes, ANDREW. This concludes your Librarian Consultation. Next? How may I help you, MIGUEL?"

"Not so fast," snapped Andrew. "I'm not done."

"Um, your consultation just concluded," said Miguel.

"Says who?"

"The librarian."

"MIGUEL?" said the hologram of Mrs Tobin. "What is *your* question?"

"Sorry, bro. I told you."

"She's just like Mrs Yunghans at school," snapped Peckleman. "All the librarians like you better than me!"

"Yo. Ease up."

"You'll see, Mrs Tobin! You'll all see. I'm gonna beat Miguel Fernandez, big-time! And when I win, I'm gonna tell Mr Lemoncello to fire you!"

"She's a hologram," said Miguel with a laugh. "You can't fire somebody who doesn't actually exist."

"Then I'll tell Lemoncello to pull her plug." Peckleman grabbed his magazine and stormed out of the rotunda into the lobby.

"I guess Andrew's planning on doing something with the front door," Kyle whispered to Akimi.

"Well, that's totally dumb. They already told us the way out isn't the way we came in."

"Maybe Andrew doesn't think Dr Zinchenko was telling us the truth," suggested Sierra.

116

"Come on," said Kyle, leading his team towards the closest staircase up to the first floor. Glancing over his shoulder, he watched Miguel place a slip of paper on the table in front of the semi-translucent librarian.

"This item has been temporarily removed from the Stacks, MIGUEL," said Mrs Tobin. "You will find it in a display case next to the original Winkle and Grimble scale model. Let me give you that location."

There was a grinding sound, like when movie tickets shoot up through the slot at the box office. Miguel snatched the small square of paper that popped up from the librarian's desk and spun around.

He froze the instant he saw Kyle, Akimi and Sierra sneaking around the room behind him.

24

"Hey," said Miguel, hiding the tiny square of paper behind his back. "Yo."

"Yo," said Kyle. "Whazzup?"

"Nothin'. Just, you know, workin' the puzzle."

"Yeah. Us too."

"OK. Later."

"Later."

Both boys thumped their fists on their chests like baseball players do. Miguel turned and ran for a staircase winding up to the first floor.

"Come on, you guys," said Kyle as he took off running for a different set of steps.

When Kyle, Akimi and Sierra made it up to the balcony, they watched Miguel run up to the second floor. As soon as he disappeared into a room up there, Kyle unrolled the game sketch.

"Look at the drawing, then look down at the floor," said Kyle.

"They're the same!" said Sierra.

"Exactly. A circular room with a round desk at the centre of that circle."

"Awesome," said Akimi. "And there are ten doors ringed around the balcony up here on the first floor, just like on the board game."

Kyle tapped the rendering of the spinner in the right-hand corner of the game plans. "See how the spinner is divided into ten different-coloured sections numbered zero to nine?"

"It looks like the Wonder Dome," said Akimi, "when it's not doing its kaleidoscope thing or running a video that makes you think the building is hang gliding across Alaska, which totally made me airsick."

"Well, in the game, you have to go into all ten Dewey decimal book rooms and answer a trivia question about a book. If you answer correctly, you slip a book into your bookshelf and move on to another part of the library. When you have ten books, one from each room, it's basically a race to see who can exit the library first."

"OK," said Akimi, sounding pumped. "This is good. This is major."

"Except one thing's missing," said Kyle.

"What?" asked Sierra.

"Mr Lemoncello always works a clever back-door shortcut into his games. For instance, in Family Frenzy ..."

"You can use the coal chute to slide into the millionaire's mansion at the end," said Akimi.

"Exactly. And in that castle game, Charles snuck out through the sewers. Anyway, when my brother Curtis beat me at Bibliomania . . ."

"You lost?" Akimi acted surprised.

"It happens. Occasionally. But only because Curtis used this shortcut." Kyle tapped a black square on the game diagram. "It took him straight out to the street. He beat me by one spin of the spinner."

"I don't see any black squares in the floor of our rotunda," said Akimi.

"Maybe," said Sierra, "for this new game, Mr Lemoncello put the secret square someplace besides the main room."

Kyle nodded. "And maybe to win this *new* game we need to play the *old* one."

"You're a genius!" said Akimi.

"No. My brother Curtis is the genius. I just like to play games. So, do libraries even have board games?"

"Sure," said Sierra. "I think. I mean, the library in my dad's town has them."

"Which department?" asked Akimi, pulling out her floor plan.

"Young adult."

Akimi tapped her map. "Second floor. Stairs over there."

"Let's go!" said Kyle.

But before they could take off, they heard Mr Lemoncello's voice echoing in the rotunda.

"Are you ready for your Extreme Challenge, Bridgette?"

Kyle and his teammates peered over the ledge of the balcony. Bridgette Wadge was alone in front of the librarian's desk, staring up at the ceiling.

"Yes, sir," she said.

"Are you sure?" Mr Lemoncello's voice boomed out of hidden speakers. "You still have twenty-two hours to find the exit."

"I want to go for it now, sir. Get a jump on everybody else."

"Very well. Dr Zinchenko? Reset the statues."

The ten holographic statues in their recessed nooks flickered off, leaving black and empty spaces.

"This Extreme Challenge is based on the classic Game of Authors card game," said Mr Lemoncello. "Here are the authors in your deck."

Magically, new holographic statues appeared as Mr Lemoncello rattled off the authors' names. "Charles Dickens, Raymond Chandler, Edgar Allan Poe, Agatha Christie, Patricia Highsmith, Mario Puzo, Frederick Forsyth, John Le Carré, Dashiell Hammett and Fyodor Dostoyevsky."

"He wrote *Crime and Punishment*," said Bridgette excitedly.

"Indeed he did."

"In fact," said Bridgette, "all those authors wrote crime novels."

"Correct again. However, that's the easy part. Dr Z?

How do we make this authors game ridiculously difficult enough to qualify as an Extreme Challenge?"

"Simple," the librarian's voice echoed under the dome. "You will have two minutes, Bridgette, to name four books written by each of our authors."

Kyle gulped. "That's impossible," he whispered.

"Not really," said Sierra. She was about to start rattling off titles when Mr Lemoncello said, "Go!" The sound of a ticking clock reverberated around the room.

"Um, OK," said Bridgette down on the main floor. "Agatha Christie. *Murder on the Orient Express, Ten Little Indians, Death on the Nile, The Mousetrap.*"

Somewhere, a bell dinged, and the British lady in the sensible shoes disappeared.

"Poe. *The Murders in the Rue Morgue, The Masque of the Red Death, The Purloined Letter, The Cask of Amontillado.*"

Another ding. Another statue vanished.

Bridgette kept going.

"Man," whispered Kyle, "what grade is she in? College?"

"Seventh," said Akimi, "just like us."

Bridgette Wadge kept tearing through the authors. The bell kept dinging.

But the clock kept ticking, too.

"Ten seconds," said Mr Lemoncello.

Bridgette had saved the worst for last.

"Fyodor Dostoyevsky. *Crime and Punishment.* Um,

Crime and Punishment . . . The one about the brothers . . .
The Brothers . . ."

And then she stalled.

She'd run out of gas.

A buzzer sounded.

"I'm sorry, Bridgette," said Dr Zinchenko. "But, as we advised you, the Extreme Challenges are extremely difficult. You will be going home with lovely parting gifts. Kindly hand your library card to Clarence and thank you for playing Escape from Mr Lemoncello's Library."

"That settles it," muttered Kyle. "I am *never, ever* asking for one of those Extreme Challenge dealios."

"Me neither," said Akimi.

"I might," said Sierra. "Maybe."

And then she showed Kyle and Akimi the rumpled sheet of paper where she had written down *five* book titles for all ten authors.

25

Akimi grabbed the door handle to the Young Adult Room. "It's locked."

"Here," said Sierra. "Use my library card."

"Huh," said Akimi. "Your books on the back are different, too."

"I think they all are. I got *The Egypt Game* and *The Westing Game*."

"Two books about games?" said Kyle. "Sweet."

Akimi slipped Sierra's card into a reader slot above the doorknob. The door clicked. Kyle pushed it open.

The walls of the Young Adult Room were painted purple and yellow. There were swirly zebra-print rugs on the floor and a lumpy cluster of beanbag chairs. A couple of sofas were designed to look like Scrabble trays, with letter-square pillows.

Akimi nudged Kyle in the ribs. "Check it out."

In the far corner stood a carnival ticket booth with a mechanical dummy seated inside. A "Fun & Games" banner hung off the booth's striped roof. The dummy inside the glass booth?

He looked like Mr Lemoncello.

He wasn't wearing a turban, but the Mr Lemoncello mannequin reminded Kyle of the Zoltar Speaks fortune-teller booths he'd seen in video game arcades.

"That's not really him, is it?" said Akimi, who was right behind Kyle.

"No. It's a mechanical doll."

The frozen automaton was dressed in a black top hat and a bright red ringmaster jacket. Since the booth had the "Fun & Games" banner, Kyle figured you might have to talk to the dummy to get a game.

"Um, hello," he said. "We'd like to play a board game."

Bells rang, whistles whistled and chaser lights blinked. The mechanical Mr Lemoncello jostled to life.

"If you want a game, just say its name." The life-size puppet's blocky jaw flapped open and shut – almost in sync with the words.

"Do you have Mr Lemoncello's Bewilderingly Baffling Bibliomania?"

"Did Joey Pigza lose control? Was Ella enchanted?"

"Huh?"

"Just say yes," suggested Sierra.

"Yes," said Kyle.

"Well, great Gilly Hopkins," said the Lemoncello dummy, "here you go!"

Kyle heard some mechanical noises and some whirring. Then, with a clunk, a wide slot popped open in the front of the booth and a game box slid out.

"Enjoy!" said the dummy. "And remember, it's not whether you win or lose, it's how you play the game. So be sure to read the instructions – so you'll know how to *play the game*."

Kyle took the box to a table.

"OK," he said, raising the lid, "let's set it up and –"

There was a beep and the door opened . . .

"Where is he?"

Andrew Peckleman barged into the room waving his antique magazine – something called *Popular Science Monthly*.

"Who're you looking for?" said Kyle.

"Mr Lemoncello. I heard him. Is he in here?"

Kyle pointed towards the frozen Lemoncello doll sitting in the carnie booth. "It's a dummy."

Peckleman whipped his head around from side to side. "Is there a camera in here?"

"Right over the door."

Peckleman spun around to face it. Kyle, Akimi and Sierra formed a human shield to hide their Bibliomania box.

"I want to use a second lifeline!" Peckleman shouted at the camera. "I want to talk to an expert!"

"Very well," said a calm voice Kyle immediately recognized as belonging to Dr Zinchenko. "With whom do you wish to speak?"

"The guy who wrote this stupid magazine article about cracking open bank vaults in the 1930s!"

"I'm afraid we cannot arrange that for you, Andrew."

"Why not? The guy's a moron. He didn't tell me anything about how to open the front door, which is what my Google search said this magazine would do!"

"We told you the way out isn't the way in."

"That was just a red herring! A trick, to throw us off course."

"No, Andrew. It was not. What is the title of the article?"

" 'Newest Bank Vaults Defy the Cracksman.' "

"Ah. Well, that should have been a hint. Apparently, the reporter concluded that thieves could *not* break open the vault doors. When doing internet research, it is important to –"

"Let me talk to the stupid idiot!"

"I am sorry. That magazine was published in 1936. The reporter is dead."

"Well, then, I want to talk to Mr Lemoncello!"

"Excuse me?"

"I want to talk to Mr Lemoncello!"

"This is highly irregular . . ."

"And so's this game. You people have it rigged so

Miguel Fernandez will win. I know you do! That's why Mr Lemoncello is afraid to talk to me."

Kyle heard the carnival booth dummy clatter back to life.

"Hello, Andrew. How may I help you?"

This Lemoncello didn't sound prerecorded. Apparently, the real deal was using the dummy to do his talking.

"Your library stinks!" shouted Peckleman.

"Oh, dear. Have you boys been playing that castle sewer game again?"

"No! But this stupid article should've given me the stupid answer but the stupid writer didn't write what he should've written."

"I see. And can you rephrase that in the form of a question?"

"How many can I ask you?"

"Just one. And then we're done."

"OK. You're the expert on this stupid new library game. So where's your favourite contestant? Where's Miguel?"

"Is that your final question?"

"Yes!"

"Assuming our video monitors are correct, Mr Fernandez is on the other side of the second floor, doing research in the Art and Artifacts Room."

"Thanks!"

Andrew bolted out the door.

The Lemoncello puppet bucked and drooped into its "off" mode.

Kyle sprang up from the table. "Come on," he said to Akimi and Sierra.

Akimi sighed. "*Now* where are we going?"

"To make sure Peckleman doesn't do something stupid that gets Miguel kicked out of the game."

"And why would we do that?"

"Because Miguel's our friend."

Akimi glanced at her floor plan. "The Art and Artifacts Room is on the other side of the circle."

"Sierra – stay here and guard the game box. Come on, Akimi."

Kyle and Akimi looped around the second-floor balcony to the other side. Kyle glanced at his watch. It was almost 3 p.m. They really needed to start focusing on The Game and not all this other monkey junk.

As they neared the Art & Artifacts Room, there was a shout, and the door flew open. Andrew Peckleman came running out.

Behind him were a woman with the head and tail of a lioness, and a Pharaoh in a cobra headpiece.

The Pharaoh stopped. "May onions grow in your earwax!" And a series of holographic hieroglyphics danced across the air.

Andrew Peckleman raced to a staircase, grabbed both handrails, and hurried down to the first floor. The Egyptians vanished.

Kyle and Akimi entered the Art & Artifacts Room and found Miguel seated at a desk with what looked like blueprints.

"You OK?" asked Kyle.

"Yeah, man. I'm fine. Thanks."

"Those guys chasing Andrew. Where'd they come from?"

"Holograms from the giant Lego Sphinx and Pyramid exhibit."

"So why'd they turn on Andrew?" asked Akimi.

"I don't know. One minute he's yelling at me. The next, the Pharaoh and Sekhmet are yelling at him."

"Sek-who?" said Kyle.

"Sekhmet," said Akimi. "The Egyptian lion goddess and warrior. Haven't you read *The Red Pyramid* by Rick Riordan?"

"It's on my list," said Kyle. Or it would be. He definitely needed to start a reading list soon so he could catch up with everybody else.

"I bet the security guards in the control room fired up the Egyptian holograms when they saw Andrew going berserk in here," said Akimi.

"Good," said Miguel. "A library is supposed to be a place for peaceful contemplation."

That was when Sierra Russell rushed into the room.

"You guys! Right after you left! The Mr Lemoncello dummy spit out a bonus card!"

26

"Very clever," said Charles, pulling another silhouette card out of a book.

This cover had been easy to find. It was the third book on the top shelf of the Staff Picks display. The image on the front was a bright yellow yield sign. The title? *Universal Road Signs* by "renowned trafficologist" Abigail Rose Painter. Charles had found the matching book in the 300s room on the first floor. The 300s were all about social sciences, including things like commerce, communications and – ta-da! – transportation.

The image also fit nicely with the pictogram he had found in the 700s room in a book called *The Umpire Strikes Back*. That baseball book was the first cover on the *second* shelf in the display case and had given Charles a card with the classic pose of an umpire calling an out.

Reading the images from left to right, then down – just like you'd read a book – Charles knew he was on the right track. The traffic sign book gave him "walk" and the umpire book gave him "out".

Put the two picture words together and he had "walk out."

Clearly, if he could find all twelve silhouettes, the Staff Picks display would tell him how to "walk out" of the library (although he had absolutely no idea what the first image he had found, the quarterback tossing a pass, had to do with escaping the library – not yet, anyway).

"Three down, nine to go," said Charles, winking up at the closest security camera. "And, Mr Lemoncello, if you're watching, may I just say that you are an extremely brilliant man?"

Charles had never sucked up to a video camera before. He figured it was worth a shot. Maybe Mr Lemoncello would send him a bonus clue or something.

Instead, when Charles stepped out of the 300s room, somebody sent him Andrew Peckleman. The goggle-eyed library geek was sputtering mad as he rushed down the steps and stomped around the first-floor balcony.

"Stupid library. Stupid Lemoncello. Stupid sphinx and Sekhmet."

"Why so glum, Andrew?" Charles called out.

"Because this game stinks. Mr Lemoncello just sent a bunch of holograms hurling hieroglyphics after me. He could put somebody's eye out with those things."

"Really? With a hologram?"

"Hey, they're made with lasers, aren't they?"

"Indeed. Say, speaking of hieroglyphics, where might I find a book about picture languages?"

"Ha! Why should I help you?"

"Because Kyle Keeley is working with Akimi Hughes *and* Sierra Russell. I imagine it is only a matter of time before your friend Miguel Fernandez joins their team, too."

"Miguel isn't my friend! Besides, I'm better at navigating my way through a library than he'll ever be."

"I know. That's why I want you on my team."

"Really?"

Charles smiled. Kids like Andrew Peckleman were so easy to manipulate.

"Oh, yes. Work with me and I guarantee you the

133

world will know that *you* should be the head library aide at Alexandriaville Middle School."

"The four hundreds!" blurted Peckleman.

"Pardon?"

"That's where you'll find books on hieroglyphics and all kinds of languages. If you want secret codes, those are in the six hundreds room. The six-fifties, to be exact."

Charles shot out his hand. "Welcome to Team Charles, Andrew."

The new teammates stepped into the 400s room. For some reason, it was pitch dark and smelled like pine trees.

"*Bienvenida! Bienvenue! Witamy! Kuwakaribisha!* Welcome!" boomed a voice from the ceiling speakers. "This is the four hundreds room, home of foreign languages. Here, CHARLES and ANDREW, you can learn all about your American heritage."

A bank of spotlights thumped on.

Charles and Andrew were face-to-blank-face with a row of four featureless mannequins. An overhead projector beamed a movie on to dummy number two, turning it into a perky woman who looked like a flight attendant.

"Hello, and welcome to *your* American heritage. I'm Debbie. Let's begin your voyage!"

"That's OK," said Charles. "We're rather busy."

"Let's begin your voyage," the mannequin repeated.

Charles sighed. Obviously, there was no way to turn

this silly display off. He might as well speed things along by telling the dummy what it wanted to hear.

"Fine. But can we go with the abridged version? We're in a bit of a rush."

"Yeah," added Andrew, "we have to escape before noon tomorrow."

The woman, whose body remained frozen while a movie made her face and costume spring to life, reminded Charles of the graveyard statues from the Haunted Mansion ride at Disney World.

"While we research your family trees," she said, "please enjoy this short and informative film."

"Is this part of the game?" Andrew whispered to Charles.

"Possibly. Pay attention for any bonus clues."

"OK. What do they look like?"

"Who can ever say?"

A screen behind the life-size dummies leapt to life with all sorts of scratchy images of people huddled together on the deck of a boat near the Statue of Liberty.

"For decades," narrated the ceiling voice, "public libraries have proudly served America's newest citizens – the immigrants who flock to these shores yearning for the freedom to build their own American dreams."

Charles really wasn't interested in this kind of stuff. His ancestors were all *Americans;* the only language they spoke was English.

"Yes, the library is where many new arrivals journey

first. To learn their new homeland's language. To keep in touch with the world they left behind. To search for the gainful employment that will make them productive residents of their newly adopted home!"

The movie dissolved into blackness.

"Thank you for your kind attention," chirped the cheerful Debbie. "We have completed your American family tree. Let's meet your first American ancestors!"

Two mannequins sprang to illuminated life, both of them dressed in traditional Thanksgiving pilgrim costumes.

"I know who they are already," said Charles. "That's John Chiltington and his wife, Elinor. They came to Plymouth Colony on the *Mayflower*. Can we move on to Andrew's family? Please?"

"Of course," said Debbie.

The mannequins quickly went through Andrew Peckleman's ancestry. Apparently, the family name had originally been Pickleman, because they made pickles. After a prolonged parade of pickle people, the dummies took on the guise of Andrew's most famous ancestor, a guy in horn-rimmed glasses and a tweed sports coat named Peter Paul Peckleman.

"I appeared on the TV game show *Concentration* in 1968," he announced, "and won a roomful of furniture and wood panelling for my rumpus room."

Charles smiled. He knew the TV game show *Concentration* was very similar to Mr Lemoncello's Phenomenal

Picture Word Puzzler, one of the games he had picked up at the toy store. Peter Paul Peckleman's claim to fame was further confirmation that piecing together the picture puzzle would show Charles how to escape from the library.

He'd been right.

The dummies had just given him a bonus clue.

27

Excited by the sudden appearance of a second bonus card, Sierra read it out loud:

"'Two plus two can equal more than four. Put two and two together and you'll be closer than before.'"

Akimi raised her hand.

"Yes?" said Sierra.

"You do realize that Miguel here isn't on our team?"

"Oh. Right. Sorry."

Miguel turned to Kyle. "You guys are a team?"

"Yep. You want to join?"

"Maybe. Not sure. Check back with me later, man."

"No problem," said Kyle.

He fist-thumped his chest. Miguel fist-thumped his. They were flashing each other peace signs when Sierra said, "I think this means we should all play together as a team. Remember what it says on the fountain down in the lobby: 'Knowledge not shared remains unknown.' "

"Maybe," said Miguel. "Like I said – let me get back to you guys. I'm workin' on a few angles of my own. Flying solo."

"Sure. No problem." Kyle was about to do the whole fist-chest-bump-peace-sign thing again when he had a brainstorm. "Miguel? Quick question. What's on your library card?"

Miguel shrugged. "My name and the number one."

"Anything else? Like on the back?"

"Nothing really. Couple of books."

"Two?"

"Yeah."

"What're their titles?"

Miguel bit his lip. "Don't want to say."

"Because you think they might be clues?"

"Not saying what I might or might not be thinking, bro."

Kyle nodded.

"There are two different books on the back of everybody's library cards," said Akimi, thinking out loud. " 'Put two and two together and you'll be closer than before.' The book titles *are* some sort of clue. My books are *One* –"

"Um, Akimi?" Kyle shook his head. Nodded towards Miguel.

"Right. Sorry. My bad."

"OK . . . Miguel," said Kyle. "If and when you decide to team up with us, you can show us the two books on the back of your card; we'll all show you ours. We'll also split the prize four ways. Deal?"

"Deal."

"Come on, guys." Kyle gestured towards the exit.

"Where are we going?" asked Sierra.

Kyle dropped his voice. "The Electronic Learning Centre."

"You want to play video games?" said Akimi. "Now? Seriously, Kyle, we may need to rethink your status as team captain."

"I don't want to play video games. I want to check out the discard pile."

"Huh?"

"The cards the players who went home early dumped into that goldfish bowl!"

"I'm comin' with you guys," said Miguel. "I've been thinking about those extra cards, too."

"Fine," said Kyle. "Whatever."

When they entered the game room, they saw Clarence, his arms folded across his chest genie-style. He was standing guard in front of the discard pile.

"May I help you?" he asked.

"Um, yeah," said Kyle. "We want to check out the cards in the bowl."

"Sorry," said Clarence. "You can't have them."

"But," said Mr Lemoncello, his face suddenly appearing on every video screen in the room, "you can win them!"

Dressed in a polka-dotted bow tie and snazzy jacket like a game show host, Mr Lemoncello had one arm resting on a slender Plexiglas podium. Behind him, Dr Zinchenko – all decked out in a sparkly red minidress – looked like the models that point at prizes on TV.

"Are the four of you ready to play Let's Do a Deal?" When Mr Lemoncello said that, he pushed a big red button in his podium. A prerecorded studio audience whistled, cheered, and applauded.

"Um, what's Let's Do a Deal?" asked Kyle.

"My first game to ever be turned into a TV show. Brought to you by lemon Pledge!"

Dr Zinchenko started singing: *"Lemon Pledge, very pretty. Put the shine down, lemon good . . ."*

"Thank you, Dr Z!" said Mr Lemoncello, bopping the button to make the audience cheer again. "Now then, kids, here's the deal: solve one simple picture puzzle and you four win the five library cards in the bowl."

"And if we lose?"

"Simple. Each of you loses his or her library card and adds it to the discard bowl for our next lucky contestants to try and win."

He banged the red button again. The audience cheered exactly the same way they cheered before.

Kyle turned to the others. "What do you say, guys?"

"Let's go for it," said Akimi.

Sierra nodded.

"Miguel?"

"I'm in, bro."

"You're joining our team?"

"Absolutely." They knocked knuckles to seal the deal.

Mr Lemoncello must've whacked his button again, because the canned studio audience started cheering.

Kyle wondered what the sound effects would be if he and his friends lost their library cards playing Let's Do a Deal.

Probably groans.

And weeping. Lots and lots of weeping.

28

"Now then," said Mr Lemoncello, "are you ready to play Risking Everything for Five Little Library Cards?"

Kyle swallowed hard. Then he nodded.

"All right, you Maniac Magees, here is your picture puzzle. The category is Famous Quotes. You have sixty seconds to solve this rebus."

"Wait a second," said Akimi. "What's a rebus?"

"You figure out the words in a phrase by looking at pictures and symbols," said Kyle.

"For instance," added Miguel, "the letters 'R' and 'E' plus a picture of a school bus would equal 'rebus'."

"Oh. OK," said Akimi. "If you guys say so."

"Are you ready to play?" asked Mr Lemoncello.

Kyle looked at his teammates, who nodded.

"Yes, sir."

"Then on your mark . . . get set . . . go, dog, go!"

Mr Lemoncello's image disappeared. Ticktock clock music started playing. The video screens all projected the same picture:

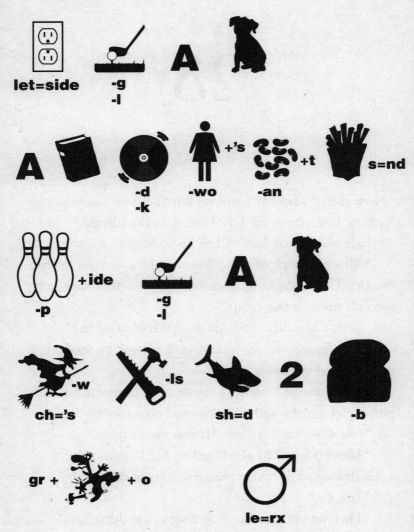

"We're officially dead," said Akimi.

"Fifty-five seconds," said Mr Lemoncello.

"OK, we break it up four ways," said Kyle. "The first and third rows are similar, I'll do them."

"I'll do the last one," said Akimi.

"I'll take the second row," said Miguel.

"I'm four," said Sierra.

"Fifty seconds," said Mr Lemoncello.

Everyone went to work.

"Mine is some guy hitting himself in the thumb but with a 'gr' and an 'o'?" muttered Akimi. "Then the male symbol where the 'le' equals 'rx'? 'Marx'? Does that make sense? Hello? Kyle? Is my second half 'Marx'?"

Kyle didn't answer. He was too busy deciphering his own clue lines. "'Outlet', change the 'let' to 'side'," he mumbled. "'Golf' minus the 'g' and the 'l'. The letter 'A'."

"Forty seconds."

"'Dog'." He dropped to the third line. He just needed the first word. "'Bowling *pins*' without the 'p' but add an 'ide.'"

"Thirty seconds."

Kyle glanced at Miguel. He was moving his lips, mouthing out his part of the quote. Sierra, too.

"You guys ready?" Kyle whispered.

"Hang on," said Miguel.

"Twenty seconds."

"OK. Go."

Kyle read the first line: "'Outside of a dog . . .'"

Miguel picked up the thread: "'. . . a book is man's best friend.'"

Kyle continued. "'Inside of a dog . . .'"

Sierra took over. "'. . . it's too dark to read.'"

Akimi brought them home: "'Groucho Marx!'"

"Is that your final answer?" asked Mr Lemoncello.

"Yes," said Kyle, and then he repeated the entire quote: "'Outside of a dog, a book is man's best friend. Inside of a dog, it's too dark to read.' – Groucho Marx."

Bells rang. Chaser lights flashed. The audience went wild. Akimi and Sierra actually squealed and hugged each other.

"You are correct!" shouted Mr Lemoncello. "There's no dead end in Norvelt, not today! Take those five library cards, Team Kyle! You won them fair and square!"

Charles and Andrew heard a commotion on the second floor. Bells ringing. An audience whooping it up. Girls squealing.

"Come on," said Charles.

They raced up the stairs and peeked into the Electronic Learning Centre. Kyle Keeley and his teammates were all hugging each other and slapping high fives. On every video screen in the game room, Charles could see a pictogram puzzle.

"What's going on in there?" whispered Andrew.

"They might be gaining on us," Charles whispered back. "We need to pick up our pace. Quick – where would I find a book called *Hoosier Hospitality* written by Eve Healy Aresty?"

"The nine hundreds room."

"Let's go."

Charles and Andrew scurried back to the first floor and the 900s room.

Where they found Haley Daley holding *Hoosier Hospitality* by Eve Healy Aresty.

"Oh, hello, you guys," she said, slamming the book shut.

Charles moved towards her. Slowly.

"Find anything interesting in that book, Haley?"

"Not really." She giggled. "Just a bunch of dumb junk about Indiana."

Charles knew she was hiding something.

"I wonder, Haley, if you and I might share a quiet word?" He turned to Andrew. "In private."

"Does that mean I'm supposed to leave?"

"Yes, Andrew. It's for the good of the team. Trust me."

"OK. But I'll be right outside that door if you decide to double-cross me or something."

"Thank you, Andrew. This will only take a quick minute."

Peckleman left the room.

Smiling, Charles moved even closer to Haley. So close he could smell her bubble gum. Or shampoo. Maybe both.

"Let's step over here," he said, taking Haley by the elbow. "I found another fascinating book that I think you'll just love." He guided her to a spot behind a bookcase where their conversation couldn't be observed by the security camera blinking up in the ceiling.

Haley went with Charles.

If he had been looking for the same book she'd just found, that meant he was playing the library escape game along a similar path. Charles Chiltington might have clues Haley could use. Clues she needed.

"Rumour has it," Charles whispered, "that your parents wrote your library essay for you."

Inside, Haley was grinning. Obviously, Charles would try to bully her into joining his team. Fine. She'd pretend to be frightened.

"What?" she whispered back, pretending to be terrified. "That's a lie. My dad just helped me with some of the spelling."

"Aha! So you admit it. All the spelling in your essay wasn't your own?"

OK. This was going to take more acting skill than usual. Having someone check your spelling wasn't against anybody's rules for anything.

She widened her eyes. Made her lips quiver. "What do you want, Charles?"

"For you to join my team."

"Why should I do that?"

"Two reasons. One, if you're on my side, your flagrant plagiarism remains our dirty little secret. Two, I know what to do with that silhouette card you just found in the *Hoosier Hospitality* book."

"You do?"

"Oh, yes. If we share our clues, the pictures will create a phrase telling us how to find the alternate exit."

Haley smiled. For real. This was working out perfectly. She'd get all their clues, and even if they all won together, Mr Lemoncello would definitely make her the real star of his TV commercials. She had "zazz". Charles and Andrew did not.

"OK," she said. "Deal. I'm on your team."

Then she handed Charles the clue she had found in the *Hoosier* book:

"Of course!" said Charles. "After all, Indiana is the Hoosier State."

29

"Oh, man," said Kyle, leading his team around the balcony, back to the Young Adult Room. "Nine library cards. This is fantastic!"

They gathered around a table.

"OK, guys. Time for everybody to put their cards on the table. Literally."

The teammates set down their cards. Kyle spread out the five from the discard bowl. Akimi pulled out a pad and wrote all the information on one master list:

BOOKS/AUTHORS ON THE BACKS OF
LIBRARY CARDS

#1 Miguel Fernandez
Incident at Hawk's Hill by Allan W. Eckert/
No, David! by David Shannon

#2 Akimi Hughes
One Fish Two Fish Red Fish Blue Fish
by Dr Seuss/Nine Stories by J. D. Salinger

#3 UNKNOWN

#4 Bridgette Wadge
Tales of a Fourth Grade Nothing
by Judy Blume/Harry Potter and the
Philosopher's Stone by J. K. Rowling

#5 Sierra Russell
The Egypt Game by Zilpha Keatley Snyder/
The Westing Game by Ellen Raskin

#6 Yasmeen Smith-Snyder
Around the World in Eighty Days
by Jules Verne/The Yak Who Yelled Yuck
by Carol Pugliano-Martin

#7 Sean Keegan
Olivia by Ian Falconer/Unreal! by Paul Jennings

#8 UNKNOWN

#9 Rose Vermette
All-of-a-Kind Family by Sydney Taylor/
Scat by Carl Hiaasen

#10 Kayla Corson
Anna to the Infinite Power
by Mildred Ames/Where the Sidewalk
Ends by Shel Silverstein

#11 UNKNOWN

#12 Kyle Keeley
I Love You, Stinky Face by Lisa McCourt/
The Napping House by Audrey Wood

"Wow," said Sierra. "That's a lot of good books. But what do all those authors and titles mean?"

"It means we need Charles's, Andrew's and Haley's cards," said Kyle.

"Really?" said Akimi. "Because if you ask me, we already have way too much information."

"Well," said Kyle, "maybe later we'll find a clue that'll tell us how to read *this* clue."

"And how are we going to do that?" asked Miguel.

"Have you ever played this?" Kyle pointed to the Bibliomania box.

"Nope. Always wanted to."

"We were just about to get up a game."

"Does this have anything to do with finding our way out of the library?"

"We sure hope so," said Akimi.

"Awesome."

"By the way," Kyle said to Miguel, "what'd you find in the Art and Artifacts Room?"

"Yeah," said Akimi. "All those papers you kept trying to hide from us."

Miguel grinned. "The original blueprints for the Gold Leaf Bank building."

"Clever," said Kyle. "That way you could look for old exits that might still exist behind new walls."

"Exactly."

"Find any extra exits?" asked Akimi.

"Nope. No hidden windows, either."

"Yeah, what's up with that? How come they built this place with so few windows?"

"To discourage bank robbers, I guess," said Kyle.

"Yep," said Miguel. "The only way in was through the front door. The fire exits could only be opened from the inside, like at a movie theatre. The vault itself was all the way down in the basement."

"Mr Lemoncello kept all that security," said Kyle, "and added his own."

"So it would seem."

"Well, hopefully Bibliomania will lead us to some kind of alternate exit."

"And fast," said Akimi. "Don't forget, we're not the only ones playing this game. One of those other guys is probably halfway out the door already."

"OK," said Kyle, "game play is pretty simple. You spin the spinner and advance your piece the number of

153

spaces the needle points to. You move around the library and go into each of the ten Dewey decimal rooms, where you can pick up a book by answering a clue card. If you guess wrong, you get a new clue card in the same room on your next turn. The first person to fill the ten slots in their 'bookshelf' and spin their way out of the library wins."

"It's sort of like Trivial Pursuit," said Sierra. "And the questions aren't all that hard because they're mostly multiple-choice."

"Let's hear one!" said Miguel eagerly.

The cards were separated into ten multicoloured mini-stacks, one for each room. Kyle grabbed a green card.

"OK, this is for the eight hundreds room. Literature. 'Deathly ill and pursued by the Ringwraiths, Frodo Baggins was carried safely across the River Bruinen on the gleaming white elf-horse of Glorfindel named: A) Asphodel, B) Asfaloth, C) Almarian, D) Anglachel'."

Akimi shook her head like she was having a brain freeze. "Wha-huh?"

"I think the answer might be 'A'," said Miguel.

"They're all 'A's,' " said Kyle. "Asphodel, Asfaloth, Al –"

"It's 'B) Asfaloth,' " said Sierra. "It's from J. R. R. Tolkien's *Lord of the Rings*."

Kyle flipped the card over and read the answer. " 'You are correct. You get a copy of *Lord of the Rings* to put in your bookshelf.' "

"So, Kyle," said Akimi, "how exactly is knowing the name of an elf-horse going to help us get out of the library?"

"Maybe it's like a secret code," suggested Miguel. "And the ten book titles will form a sentence telling us how to get out."

"Possibly," said Kyle. "But I see one problem."

"What's that?"

"It's too random. Mr Lemoncello would have no idea which ten cards we might pick."

"Well," said Sierra, "maybe there are only *ten* questions. One for each room."

Akimi grabbed the card stacks, fanned them out. "Nope. They're all different."

"Hang on," said Kyle.

He was remembering something about another game: Mr Lemoncello's Indoor-Outdoor Scavenger Hunt.

How his mother had been able to write to the company and request a fresh set of cards.

He turned to the video camera mounted in a corner. "I'd like my Librarian Consultation, please."

"What's up, Kyle?" asked Miguel.

"I'm playing a hunch."

The holographic Mrs Tobin appeared behind the young adult librarian's desk.

"How may I help you, KYLE?"

"My friends and I want to play Bibliomania but we were wondering: Is there a new set of cards?"

"Yes, KYLE. There is."

And a fresh deck of cards popped up through a slot in the desk.

30

"We'll just play one bookshelf," said Kyle.

"Because we're a team now, right, bro?" said Miguel.

"Right. Plus, we don't have all day."

"Well," said Akimi, "technically we do. In fact, we have the rest of today and tomorrow till noon."

"We've got like nineteen hours left," said Miguel.

"But Charles and the others," said Sierra. "They could beat us."

"Right," said Kyle. "After all, he *is* a Chiltington. And according to Sir Charles, they never lose. Miguel, you're the newest member of the team. You spin first."

Miguel rubbed his hands together. Limbered up his fingers. Practiced flicking his index finger off his thumb. Made sure he had a good snap and follow-through.

"Would you hurry up and spin before my brain explodes?" pleaded Akimi.

"No problem." Miguel flicked the plastic pointer. It whirled around the cardboard square decorated with a sunburst of ten colourful triangles.

"Boo-yah! The triple zeros. General Knowledge."

"Um, that's not so great," said Kyle.

"How come?"

"You get to move zero spaces."

"Oh. Bummer."

Akimi shot up her hand.

"Yes?" said Kyle.

"Do we really have to spin and count spaces and all that junk? We have a deadline. Clocks everywhere are ticking against us."

"Maybe we can just pull a pink card," suggested Sierra.

"It's really not how you play the game," said Kyle.

"Um, we're not really playing this game, Kyle," said Akimi. "We're playing the other one. The Big Game. The one with the ginormous prize."

"I have to agree with Akimi," said Miguel.

"Fine," said Kyle. "It's against the rules, but pull a pink card."

"You sure, bro?"

"Just pull a pink!"

Miguel quickly sorted the new deck into ten stacks of different colours. He pulled the pink on the top of its pile.

"Hmmm. These are different from the regular cards."

He turned it over and showed it to the group.

$0 + 27 + 0.4 = ????$

"Easy-peasy," said Akimi. "The answer is twenty-seven-point-four, because the zero doesn't change the sum."

"Not in math," said Miguel. "But this isn't math. This is the Dewey decimal system and there's always three numbers to the left of the decimal point."

"We need to find a book with the call number 027.4," added Sierra.

"Fine," said Akimi. "But I guarantee you it isn't a math book!"

The team made their way around the balcony circling the Dewey decimal doors.

"Here we go," said Miguel. He slid his library card into a reader on a door labelled "000s".

"OK," said Miguel, "in here we're gonna find General Knowledge. Almanacs, encyclopaedias, bibliographies, books about library science . . ."

"It's a science?" said Akimi. "Where do they keep the chemicals?"

"In the library paste," joked Sierra, who was loosening up. She hadn't read one page of a book in hours.

"Found it," said Miguel, reaching up to pull a book off a shelf. "027.4. Man, it's old. Look how yellow the pages are."

"So what's the antique's title?" asked Akimi.

"*Get to Know Your Local Library* by Amy Alessio and Erin Downey."

Miguel held the book so everybody could see the cover. It was illustrated with a cartoony-looking detective in a checkered hat who was holding up a magnifying glass to examine books on a shelf.

"Looks like a library guide for kids," said Miguel, opening the cover to read one of the inside pages. "First publication was way back in 1952." He flipped through a few pages. "It explains the Dewey decimal system. Contains a glossary of library terms. A brief history of libraries . . ."

He reached the back of the book.

"Awesome."

"What?" asked Kyle as he and the others moved closer to see what Miguel had found.

"It's an old-fashioned book slip. From the Alexandria-ville Public Library."

"The one they tore down?"

"Yep. And this card, tucked into a sleeve glued to the back cover, comes from the olden days when they used to stamp the date the book was due on a grid and you had to fill in your name under 'issued to.'"

"And?"

"Look who checked this book out on 26 May '64!"

Kyle and the others looked.

"Luigi Lemoncello!"

*   *   *

Down on the ground floor, Charles used his library card to open the door to Community Meeting Room A.

"Who is to have access to this room?" cooed a soothing voice from the ceiling.

"Me and my teammates," said Charles. "Andrew Peckleman and Haley Daley."

"Thank you. Please have ANDREW PECKLEMAN and HALEY DALEY swipe their cards through the reader now."

Both of them did.

"Thank you. Entrance to Community Meeting Room A will be limited to those approved by the host, CHARLES CHILTINGTON. Have a good meeting."

Charles and his team entered the sleek, ultramodern, white-on-white conference room. There were twelve comfy chairs set up around a glass-topped table and a cabinet filled with top-of-the-line audiovisual equipment.

"You can write on the walls," said Andrew. "They're like the Smart Boards at school."

"Excellent," said Charles, clasping his hands behind his back and pacing around the room. "Now, when we find all twelve pictograms and lay them out according to their position in the Staff Picks display case, they will create a rebus for a phrase that, I am quite certain, will tell us exactly how to exit this library without triggering any alarms. Therefore, it is time for all of us to lay our cards on the table."

Haley nodded. And pulled two more silhouettes out of the back pocket of her jeans.

"I found one of these in a cookbook," she said. "The other was in juvenile fiction. *Nancy Drew: The Mystery at Lilac Inn*."

"There are blank note cards in this drawer," announced Andrew. "We should use them as placeholders for the books we still need to find."

They laid out a three-by-four grid of cards on the tabletop:

"What does it mean?" said Andrew.

"Simple," said Charles. "It means we need to find those other six books!"

31

"So, does anybody have a clue as to why we were supposed to find this book?" asked Kyle.

He and his teammates were back in the Young Adult Room staring at the cover of *Get to Know Your Local Library*.

"Too early to tell," said Miguel. "Let's keep playing. This book will probably make more sense once we go into the other rooms and pick up more clues."

"Whose turn is it?" asked Akimi.

"Yours," said Kyle. "Flick the spinner."

Akimi finger-kicked the plastic pointer.

"Purple!" she yelled when the arrow slid to a stop. "The eight hundreds."

"That means you move eight spaces," mumbled Kyle.

"Except today." Akimi reached for the card on top of

the purple stack. When she saw what was written on it, she frowned.

"What's the clue?" asked Kyle.

"Something about Literature, Rhetoric or Criticism?" asked Miguel.

"Nope," said Akimi. "It's a wild card. With a riddle."

"Read it!" said Sierra.

" 'I rhyme with dart and crackerjacks. Visit me and find a rhyme for Andy.' "

"Peckleman?" said Kyle. "How'd he get his name on a game card?"

"Bro," said Miguel, "nobody calls Andrew Peckleman 'Andy'. Of course, it could mean Andrew Jackson. The seventh president of the United States."

"Or Andy Panda," said Akimi.

"Or Andrew Carnegie," said Sierra. "He was a generous supporter of libraries."

"OK," said Kyle. "Let's concentrate on the first part of the riddle. What rhymes with 'dart and crackerjacks'?"

"Smart and heart attacks?" suggested Miguel.

"Art and bric-a-bracs?" said Sierra.

"Art and *Artifacts*!" said Akimi, nailing it.

They hurried over to the Art & Artifacts Room.

"Everybody – check out the display cases," said Kyle. "See if anything rhymes with the word 'Andy'."

"Well, this model of the old bank building is certainly 'grandy'," said Miguel. "And the Pharaoh's pyramid and sphinx would be *sandy* if they weren't made out of Legos."

"True," said Kyle, sounding unconvinced about both.

"Check it out, you guys," cried Akimi, who was studying a row of Styrofoam heads sporting hats. "This plaid fedora from 1968 was worn by a guy named Leopold Loblolly."

"So?" said Kyle.

"According to this plaque, Loblolly was 'one of the notorious *Dandy* Bandits.' 'Dandy' rhymes with 'Andy'."

"That it does," said Miguel. "However, 'Loblolly' does not."

"Neither does 'Leopold'," added Kyle.

"'Candy' rhymes with 'Andy'!" said Sierra. She was staring at the objects in a display case under a banner reading "Welcome to the Wonderful World of Willy Wonka."

"Awesome!" said Miguel, hurrying over to admire the collection of Everlasting Gobstoppers, Glumptious Glob-gobblers, Laffy Taffy and Pixy Stix displayed under glass in a sea of purple velvet.

"Mr Lemoncello is a lot like Willy Wonka," said Kyle.

"You mean crazy?" said Akimi.

"I prefer the term 'eccentric'."

"And Dr Zinchenko is his Oompa-Loompa," said Sierra. Everybody started giggling.

"Nah," Akimi joked, "she's too tall."

164

"And not nearly orange enough," added Miguel.

"The Willy Wonka book was written by Roald Dahl," said Sierra, who, Kyle figured, could name twelve other books the guy wrote, too. "In it, Mr Wonka takes Charlie and Grandpa Joe home in a flying glass elevator that crashes through the roof of his chocolate factory."

Everybody thought about that for a second.

"So now we have to find a glass elevator?" said Akimi. "Because there isn't one on the floor plan."

"But Mr Lemoncello is just wild enough to build one," said Kyle. "And if he did, he probably wouldn't put it on the floor plan."

"No way," said Miguel. "Everybody would want to ride on it."

"I know I would," said Sierra.

"So we're seriously searching for a secret glass elevator?" said Akimi.

"Maybe," said Kyle. "Maybe not. This is just another piece of a gigantic jigsaw puzzle. We won't see the whole picture until we collect all the pieces."

"Or someone shows us the box lid," cracked Akimi.

"Look, it's only six p.m.," said Kyle. "And we're collecting a ton of good information."

"You mean a ton of *random* information," said Akimi.

"Well," said Miguel, "once we have more clues, we can use Sherlock Holmes's famous 'deductive reasoning' method to make logical connections between all the random junk."

"Works for me," said Kyle. "But if we're going to play Sherlock Holmes, we need to go spin that spinner and dig up more clues."

"The game's afoot," said Sierra.

"Huh?" Kyle and Akimi said it together.

"Sorry. It's just something Sherlock says to Watson whenever he gets excited."

Sherlock Holmes. Kyle had just found another bunch of books to add to his reading list.

32

"OK, Sierra," said Kyle, "your turn."

Sierra flicked the spinner. The pointy tip ended up in the yellow 200s zone, so she went ahead and pulled a yellow card.

"It's definitely for the two hundreds section," she said, showing her clue to Miguel before revealing it to Kyle and Akimi.

"Weird," said Miguel.

"What?" said Akimi before Kyle could.

"Well, the two hundreds are where they keep books on world religions."

"But there are *two* numbers on this card," said Sierra.

"Maybe this time we need to find *two* books?" suggested Kyle.

"I don't know," said Sierra, studying her card. " '220.5203' is obviously a call number."

"Obviously," said Akimi.

"But this other number isn't in the proper format. 'Two-twenty-fifteen.'"

"February twentieth, 2015!" said Akimi. "Quick – what happened on that date?"

"Um, that's my cousin's birthday . . ." said Kyle.

"All right . . . OK – how about February twentieth, 1915?"

"That was the opening day of the Panama-Pacific International Exposition in San Francisco," said Sierra.

Jaws dropped.

"Sorry. I'm a big world's fair fan."

Everybody else just nodded.

Finally, Miguel spoke up. "Look, let's just go down to the two hundreds room and find 220.5203. We can figure out the second chunk later."

The team once again trooped down to the first floor and worked their way around the circular balcony.

"You guys?" said Sierra, looking across the atrium at the statues. "Remember how they switched all the hologram authors when Bridgette Wadge did her Extreme Challenge?"

"Yep," said Kyle. "She was doing good till she got to the Russian dude."

"What Russian dude?" asked Miguel, who hadn't witnessed Bridgette's elimination.

"Guy who wrote five or six books Sierra could tell you about."

"But look," said Sierra. "Now all the author statues are the same ones they were last night."

"So," said Kyle thoughtfully, "if they can switch 'em around . . ."

"These must be clues for our game!" blurted Akimi. She pulled out a pen and her notepad. "I'll write down their names."

"Start with the guy under the triple zeros wedge of the Wonder Dome," suggested Kyle.

"Right."

Akimi read the labelled pedestals and jotted down all the authors' names:

Thomas Wolfe, Booker T. Washington, Stephen Sondheim, George Orwell, Lewis Carroll, Dr Seuss, Maya Angelou, Shel Silverstein, Pseudonymous Bosch, Todd Strasser.

"So," said Akimi when she'd finished writing, "do you think this game could get any more complicated?"

"Maybe," said Kyle. "It's possible that Mr Lemoncello left a couple different paths to the same solution."

"Well, personally, I can only take one path at a time," said Akimi. "So let's go find two-twenty-point-whatever."

* * *

"Should be in the next row of bookcases," said Miguel. "Here we go. 220.5203. The King James Bible."

"*Ach der lieber!* An excellent choice," said a man with a thick German accent.

The four teammates spun around.

And were face to face with a semi-transparent guy in medieval garb with a fur-trimmed cap and a beard that looked like two raccoon tails sewn together under his nose and chin.

"I am Johannes Gensfleisch zur Laden zum Gutenberg," said the holographic image, who had ink stains all over his fingertips.

"You created the Gutenberg Bibles on your printing press!" gushed Sierra.

"Ja, ja, ja. Big bestseller. You need help with der Bible, I am at your service." He bowed.

"OK . . ." said Akimi, turning to Miguel. "Take it away, Miguel."

"Herr Gutenberg, sir, we're looking for two-twenty-fifteen."

"*Das ist einfach.*"

"Huh?"

"That is easy. TWO, TWENTY, FIFTEEN is EXODUS, chapter TWENTY, verse FIFTEEN."

"Of course!" said Miguel. "Exodus is the second book of the Bible. Twenty and fifteen are the chapter and verse." He flipped through some pages. "Here we go. Exodus, chapter twenty, verse fifteen. It's one of the Ten Commandments: 'Thou shalt not steal'."

33

"Let's put the two new cards on the table," said Charles.

He and his so-called teammates, Andrew and Haley (Charles planned on dumping them both right before he made his glorious solo exit from the library), had scoured the library together for hours looking for more book cover matches.

Peckleman wasn't nearly as good with the Dewey decimal system as he had claimed to be. And Charles needed someone to do that sort of thing for him. His father always hired tutors or research assistants for him whenever Charles had to do a major paper or report.

Finally, around six in, coincidentally, the 600s room, they scored twice, finding *Tea for You and Me* (641.3372) and *Why Wait to Lose Weight?* (613.2522).

Now their picture puzzle had only four blanks remaining:

"OK," said Andrew, "I think it's pretty clear. 'Woolly BLANK walk up the skinny BLANK BLANK house Indian and nineteen BLANK'."

Charles nodded and said, "Interesting," even though he knew Peckleman was way off.

"Uh, hello?" said Haley. "That doesn't make any sense."

"Sure it does," said Andrew.

"Uh, no it doesn't."

In his head, Charles had decoded the clues so far as

"Ewe (a female sheep) BLANK walk out the (t+h+e) way (weigh) BLANK BLANK Inn in passed (past) BLANK."

But out loud, he said, "I think we just need to tweak Andrew's translation a little."

"Fine. Go ahead. I don't care." Andrew slumped down in his seat to sulk.

"How about 'She BLANK walks out the skinny BLANK BLANK house five hundred and past BLANK'?"

"Where'd you get 'she'?" asked Haley.

"From 'sheep'. The card you gave us."

"Actually, I think the sheep is supposed to represent 'you'. Because a ewe is a female sheep."

"Fascinating," said Charles. "I didn't figure that out."

What he did figure out was that Haley Daley was much smarter than he had assumed. She could be a serious threat. And no way was Charles sharing his prize with anybody, especially her.

"And how did you get 'five hundred' from Indiana?" she asked.

"Simple. Indianapolis, the capital of Indiana, is home to a race known as the Indy 500."

"OK. So how about 'You BLANK walk out the skinny BLANK BLANK in – because the Nancy Drew book was about an inn – five hundred pass, or *past,* BLANK'?"

Now Peckleman piped up. "That makes more sense than what you said, Charles."

"Indeed," said Charles, sounding magnanimous.

"Perhaps the clues are telling us to locate a secret skinny passageway five hundred paces past some landmark here in the library."

Andrew was excited. "This is like the pirate map from *Treasure Island*!"

"Or," said Haley, "maybe these clues are telling us we need to go out and find the four books we haven't found yet. We should split up. I'll go back to the four hundreds room."

"We've already been there," said Andrew.

"Well, you guys might've missed something."

"Good idea," said Charles. He figured if Haley Daley wasted time retracing steps he and Andrew had already taken, she would find nothing new and become less of a threat. "Let's meet back here at, say, seven."

"Fine."

Haley left the meeting room.

Charles went to the door and closed it.

"You know what we really need?" he said to Andrew.

"Chocolate milk and maybe some cookies?"

Charles shook his head. "No, Andrew. We need whatever clues Kyle Keeley and his team have found. Especially if they have our missing cards."

34

Veering left the instant she reached the first floor, Haley made her way towards the 400s room.

She figured that Charles and Andrew had probably missed something important in the foreign languages room because they'd spent too much time talking to "these awesome mannequins" that told them all about their "American heritage."

As she rounded the bend, Haley saw Kyle Keeley and his crew tumble out of the 200s room.

It looked like Miguel was carrying a Bible.

But a Bible wasn't one of the books on display in the Staff Picks case.

We're following separate paths to the same goal, Haley thought. *And somewhere, those two paths are going to collide.*

Haley slid her card key down the reader slot in the 400s door. The lock clicked and she pushed the door open.

The room was dimly lit.

"*Bienvenida! Bienvenue! Witamy! Kuwakaribisha!* Welcome!" boomed a voice from the ceiling speakers.

"Sorry," said Haley, blindly feeling her way forward and bumping into something hard and lumpy.

"This is the four hundreds room, home of foreign languages. Here, HALEY, you can learn all about your American heritage."

A bank of spotlights thumped on.

Haley was basically hugging a department store mannequin.

An overhead projector beamed a movie on to the dummy to her left, turning it into a perky woman who looked like Haley would probably look a couple of years after she graduated from college.

"Hello, HALEY. Welcome to *your* American heritage. Let's begin your voyage!"

"That's OK, I don't have time right now. I'm Haley Daley. My ancestors were Irish, OK? So can we skip the history lesson and . . ."

Suddenly, the two mannequins at the far end of the row turned into sepia-toned versions of her great-great-great-grandmother and great-great-great-grandfather. Haley knew it was them because her dad had a bunch of old photos hanging in their family room. The two dummies looked exactly like Patrick and Oona Daley did in their wedding portrait.

"No man ever wore a scarf as warm as his daughter's arm around his neck," said Patrick in his thick Irish brogue. "Yer da is proud of you, Haley."

"Thanks. But I really need to win this competition."

"Watch out for sneaky rascals," said Oona. "Them that would steal the sugar out of your punch."

Haley had to smile. It sounded like her ancestor had met Charles Chiltington.

"And always remember, Haley," said her great-great-great-grandfather, "every woman's mind is her kingdom. Rule it wisely, lassie."

"I'm trying!"

"This library can help," said her great-great-great-grandmother with a wink.

And when she did, a secret panel in the wall slid open.

"What's going on?" said Haley.

"You're our third visitor!" boomed the jolly announcer in the ceiling.

"So?"

"According to *The American Heritage Dictionary of Idioms* – available in our reference department, by the way – 'the third time is a charm'! Therefore, as our third visitor, you have won this charming bonus."

Two bonuses in one day?

She was right! Mr Lemoncello definitely wanted Haley Daley to win this game, because clearly he knew she'd be the perfect, best-looking spokesmodel for his holiday commercials.

"Don't worry, sir!" Haley said to the nearest TV camera. "I won't let you down."

She hurried through the open wall panel and into the 300s room on the other side.

Ta-da!

The first thing she saw was one of the books they'd been searching for all day long: *True Crime Ohio: The Buckeye State's Most Notorious Brigands, Burglars, and Bandits* by Clare Taylor-Winters.

She quickly opened the cover and found the hidden four-by-four card. It took her two seconds to decipher the clue:

"Bandits."

Haley remembered another bit of Irish wisdom, something her dad said all the time: "Never bolt your door with a boiled carrot!"

She decided to keep this new clue secret and secure. She wouldn't share it with Charles or Andrew.

Haley took off her left sneaker, folded the card in half, and slid the clue into her shoe for safekeeping. When her sneaker was laced up tight again, she took the *True Crime Ohio* book off its display stand and tucked it into the bookshelf, making sure it was in the proper position: right between 364.1091 and 364.1093. That way, she'd know where to find it if, for whatever reason, she needed the book again.

Haley looked up at the nearest camera and flashed it her brightest toothpaste-commercial smile.

"Goooo, Le-moncell-ooooo! That's a cheer I just made up. We can use it in one of the commercials – after I win!"

35

"Entrance to Community Meeting Room B will only be granted to KYLE KEELEY, SIERRA RUSSELL, AKIMI HUGHES and MIGUEL FERNANDEZ," said the soothing female voice in the ceiling after the four teammates had swiped their cards through the meeting room door's reader slot.

"This makes sense," said Akimi. "We needed a place to organize all this material, put it on the walls and draw a chart like the FBI always does on TV when they're tailing the mob."

"Stole the meeting room idea from me, eh, Keeley?"

Charles Chiltington was standing in the doorway to Meeting Room A on the far side of the rotunda.

"No," said Kyle. "We just needed someplace to throw our victory party after we win."

"Not going to happen," Charles said smugly. "Must

I remind you? I'm a Chiltington. We never lose." And he disappeared back into Meeting Room A.

After Charles was gone, Kyle led his team into Meeting Room B.

Miguel posted the bank blueprints he had found up on the walls while Sierra set up the Bibliomania board game on the conference table.

"I'm glad this room won't let anybody else in," said Kyle.

"And by 'anybody' you mean Charles Chiltington, right?" said Akimi.

"Totally."

Akimi grabbed a marker and wrote a neat outline on the dry-erase walls:

CLUES SO FAR

DEFINITE CLUES

1) From the 000s room:
Get to Know Your Local Library book

2) From the Art & Artifacts Room:
Willy Wonka candy (rhymes with "Andy").
Find glass elevator?

3) From the 200s room:
Bible verse – "Thou shalt not steal."

PROBABLY CLUES

BOOKS/AUTHORS ON THE BACKS OF LIBRARY CARDS

#1 Miguel Fernandez
Incident at Hawk's Hill by Allan W. Eckert/
No, David! by David Shannon

#2 Akimi Hughes
One Fish Two Fish Red Fish Blue Fish
by Dr Seuss/Nine Stories by J. D. Salinger

#3 UNKNOWN

#4 Bridgette Wadge
Tales of a Fourth Grade Nothing
by Judy Blume/Harry Potter and the
Philosopher's Stone by J. K. Rowling

#5 Sierra Russell
The Egypt Game by Zilpha Keatley Snyder/
The Westing Game by Ellen Raskin

#6 Yasmeen Smith-Snyder
Around the World in Eighty Days
by Jules Verne/The Yak Who Yelled Yuck
by Carol Pugliano-Martin

#7 Sean Keegan
Olivia by Ian Falconer/Unreal! by Paul Jennings

#8 UNKNOWN

#9 Rose Vermette
All-of-a-Kind Family by Sydney Taylor/
Scat by Carl Hiaasen

#10 Kayla Corson
Anna to the Infinite Power
by Mildred Ames/Where the Sidewalk
Ends by Shel Silverstein

#11 UNKNOWN

#12 Kyle Keeley
I Love You, Stinky Face by Lisa McCourt/
The Napping House by Audrey Wood

MAYBE CLUES???

Statues ringed around the dome:

Thomas Wolfe, Booker T. Washington, Stephen
Sondheim, George Orwell, Lewis Carroll,
Dr Seuss, Maya Angelou, Shel Silverstein,
Pseudonymous Bosch, Todd Strasser

"Wow," said Akimi, stepping back to study the walls. "What an incredible mess."

"Yeah," said Kyle. "OK, guys – there are eight more book rooms to explore and who knows how many more wild cards. Whose turn is it?"

"Yours," said Sierra.

Kyle flicked the spinner. "Green. The five hundreds. Science."

He pulled the first green card from the deck.

" 'Four and twenty were once in a pie. 598.367 might tell you why.' "

"Blackbirds?" said Miguel.

"I guess."

"Well," sighed Akimi, "let's go check out *another* book. There's still like an inch or two left on our whiteboard."

The 500s room was like a miniature museum of natural history.

In addition to towering walls of books, there was a whole planetarium of stars and constellations projected on the ceiling. Models of planets whirled in their orbits. Sparkle-tailed comets shot around the corners of book-shelves.

Kyle and his teammates made their way back to the 590s – Zoology.

Shelving units were arranged in a square around an open area, maybe twenty feet by twenty feet wide. When the team entered the empty space, the lights dimmed and a guy with long wavy hair who looked like an artistic Daniel Boone faded into view. He was wearing some kind of bear-fur coat and toting a musket.

"*Bonjour,*" said the hologram.

"It's John James Audubon," said Sierra. "The famous ornithologist."

"He gives people braces?" said Kyle.

"No," Sierra said with a laugh. "He studied and painted birds."

A blackbird with a yellow beak flew into the open area and roosted on a tree branch. The bird and the tree were both holograms, too.

"This beautiful blackbird from Alexandriaville, Ohio," said the semi-transparent Audubon image, "can mimic in song the sounds it has heard."

And the bird started wailing.

"Wow," said Akimi. "That sounds exactly like a police siren!"

"Yo," said Miguel. "Freaky."

"To learn more," said Audubon, "be sure to read *Bird Songs, Warbles and Whistles* written by Dr Diana Victoria Garcia, with classic illustrations by *moi.*"

With that, Audubon sat down on a campstool. An easel appeared, the blackbird struck a pose, and the outdoorsy artist started painting the bird's portrait, while humming "Blackbird" by the Beatles.

"OK," said Kyle. "This is the strangest clue yet."

"Well, here's the book at least," said Sierra, who had found 598.367 on the shelf.

"So what do a blackbird's wails and warbles have to do with finding our way out of the library?" said Akimi.

Just then, they heard a very different sound.

Behind one of the bookcases, something growled, then roared.

"Did you guys hear that?" said Sierra.

"Yeah," said Akimi. "I don't think it's a robin red-breast."

A very rare white Bengal tiger, with icy-blue eyeballs, crept out from behind a wall of bookshelves and stalked into the open area where Audubon sat painting his bird portrait.

"Uh, is that another hologram?" asked Miguel.

ROAR!

No one stuck around to find out.

36

Down on the ground floor, Charles and Andrew were working their way around the semicircle of three-story-tall floor-to-dome bookcases filled with fiction.

It was nearly 8 p.m.

"We need to find that blasted book," said Charles, craning his neck to study the shelves.

"I'm getting kind of hungry," mumbled Andrew.

"You had a snack this afternoon," snapped Charles.

"Well, now it's time for dinner."

"No. We need to find *Anne of Green Gables* first."

The classic by Lucy Maud Montgomery was the middle book on the top shelf in the Staff Picks display case. So far, Charles, Haley and Andrew had not been able to find it anywhere in the library.

"Unfortunately," said Andrew, "they've temporarily erased the book's call number from the database."

"So we wouldn't know what to punch into the hover ladder's control panel," grumbled Charles.

"Actually," said Andrew, "they might've shelved it in the Children's Room. Or maybe the eight hundreds, with Literature. Could be in the four hundreds, too, because it was originally written in Canadian, which is, technically, a foreign language."

"So you have said, Andrew. Repeatedly. But we've already searched those other locations. Several times. It has to be here with the other fiction titles. You just need to fly up and find it."

"Well," said Andrew, "I'm kind of afraid of heights."

"Fine. Whatever. I'll go up and grab it. But you have to give me some kind of call number to enter into the hover ladder."

"Lucy Maud Montgomery wrote other Anne books. There's *Anne of Avonlea . . .*"

Charles dashed over to the nearest library table and swiped his fingers across the glass face of its built-in computer pad.

"Here we go. *Anne of Avonlea* by Lucy Maud Montgomery. F-MON."

"Yes," said Andrew. "Fiction books are usually put on the shelf in alphabetical order by the author's last name. Nonfiction titles are classified according to the Dewey decimal system."

"How long have you known this?"

Andrew's nose twitched. "Since second grade."

"So all we ever needed was 'F-MON'? We could've found this book hours ago?"

Andrew gulped.

"You are such a disappointment." Shaking his head, Charles huffed over to one of the hover ladders. He quickly jabbed "F", "M", "O" and "N" into the keypad. The boot clamps locked into place around his ankles. "You owe me for wasting all this time, Andrew. You owe me big-time. If you let me down once more, I swear I will tell everybody you're a big blubbering baby. I'll Twitter it *and* post it on Facebook."

"Don't worry. I'll make you glad you picked me for your team, Charles! I promise."

The hover ladder lifted off the floor and gently glided up to the M section of the fiction wall. Shuttling sideways, it carried Charles over to a shelf displaying all the Anne books.

He grabbed a copy of *Anne of Green Gables*.

As soon as he did, the ladder started its slow descent to the floor.

"What'd you find?" asked Andrew when Charles landed.

"The clue we needed."

He showed Andrew the card that had been tucked inside the front cover.

"OK," said Andrew. "It's 'C plus hat'! So the word is 'chat', which, by the way, could also be *'chat'*, the French word for cat!"

"Well done, Andrew," said Charles, even though he knew the clue was really "C plus Anne", equalling "can", thereby making the puzzle "You *can* walk out the way BLANK BLANK inn in past BLANK."

The way what did what? he wondered. *And what does "inn in" mean?*

Charles desperately needed to find the three missing pictograms.

Suddenly, Mr Lemoncello's voice boomed out of speakers ringing the rotunda.

"Hey, Charles! Hey, Andrew! Let's Do a Deal!"

Game show music blared. A canned crowd cheered.

Charles turned around and saw shafts of coloured light illuminating three envelopes perched on top of the librarian's round desk. Clarence the security guard marched into the reading room and, folding his arms over his chest, took up a position near the three envelopes.

"We have a green envelope, a blue envelope and a red envelope," said Mr Lemoncello. "In two of those three envelopes are copies of two of the three pictogram clues you still need. In one, there is a Clunker Card. If you pick an envelope with a clue, you get to keep it – and you get to keep going. But once you pick the Clunker Card, you're done . . . and you must suffer the consequences."

Andrew raised his hand.

"Yes, Andrew?"

"What are the consequences?"

"Something bad," said Mr Lemoncello. "In fact, something wicked this way will probably come. Do you want to do a deal?"

"Yes!" said Charles.

The canned audience cheered.

"All right, then! Charles, you roll first."

"Pardon?"

"Swipe your fingers across the nearest desktop computer panel. The dice tumbler app is up and running!"

Again, the prerecorded audience cheered. They sounded like they loved watching dice tumble more than anything in the world.

Charles slid his fingers across a glass pane. The animated dice rolled.

"Oooh!" cried Mr Lemoncello. "Double sixes. That gives you a twelve."

"Is that good, sir?"

"Maybe. Maybe not. OK, Andrew – your turn!"

Peckleman tapped the glass. The dice flipped over.

"Another set of doubles!" said Mr Lemoncello.

"Yeah," muttered Charles. "Two ones. Snake eyes."

"Is that bad?" asked Andrew.

"Maybe," said Mr Lemoncello. "Maybe not. OK, guys – which envelope would you like to open?"

Charles thought about it while ticktock music played.

They were given this chance to play Let's Do a Deal

after they located the *Anne of Green Gables* clue. Coincidence? He didn't think so.

"We'll take the green envelope, sir."

Clarence presented the green envelope to Charles.

"Open it!" said Andrew. "Open it."

Charles undid the clasp. Pulled out a card.

A loud *ZONK!* rocked the room.

The card was black. With blocky white type.

"Uh-oh," mumbled Andrew. "What's it say on that card?"

" 'Sorry, kids, you're out of luck,' " read Charles. " 'So out of doors you're all now stuck.' "

Clarence picked up the blue and red envelopes and marched back towards the entrance hall.

"What's that mean?" said Andrew.

"Well," said Mr Lemoncello, "Charles rolled a twelve and you rolled a two. What's twelve plus two?"

"Fourteen," said Charles eagerly, the way he always did in math when he wanted to remind the teacher that he was the smartest kid in the class.

"Oooh," said Mr Lemoncello. "This is not good. In fact, I'd say it's stinkerrific."

"Stinkerrific?" said Andrew. "Is that even a word?"

"It is now," said Mr Lemoncello. "J.J.? Tell them what they've lost."

An authoritative female voice boomed out of the ceiling speakers:

"Warning: Due to a Clunker Card, all ten Dewey decimal doors will lock in ten minutes, at exactly eight o'clock. If you are in one of those rooms, kindly leave immediately. The ten doors on the first floor will remain locked for fourteen hours."

Andrew panicked. "What? Fourteen hours?"

"I told you twelve plus two was bad," quipped Mr Lemoncello. "Of course, it could've been good. If you had picked one of the other envelopes, you would've received a clue and a free fourteen-month subscription to *Library Journal*."

Charles did some quick math. "Sir? Does this mean we'll be locked out of the ten Dewey decimal rooms until ten o'clock tomorrow morning?"

"Bingo!" said Mr Lemoncello. "It sure does!"

"This stinks," whined Andrew. "We need those stupid rooms to solve your stupid puzzle! Clunker Cards stink. This game stinks. Fourteen-hour penalties stink."

Charles did his best to block out Andrew's rant.

He needed to think.

And then it hit him: *Kyle Keeley's team had to be working on some other solution to the bigger puzzle of how to escape from the library.* Otherwise, Charles and his team would not have been able to find the nine clues they'd already picked up. Surely, if Keeley's team had been playing the same memory match game, they would've found at least one of the pictograms before Charles, Andrew or Haley did.

They must be working a completely different angle.

Charles was certain that if he could use this downtime

to learn what Keeley and his team had in their meeting room, and combined it with his picture puzzle, he would emerge from the library victorious.

"Do not despair, Andrew," Charles said confidently. "We are still going to win."

"How?"

Charles leaned in and cupped a hand around his mouth so no security cameras could read his lips.

"Remember," he whispered, "you need to pay me back for wasting a ton of time in finding *Anne of Green Gables*."

"What? You're the one who picked the stupid green envelope with the stupid Clunker Card!"

Charles narrowed his eyes and chilled his hushed voice. "So?"

"Um, nothing," said Andrew nervously. "Just thought I'd, you know, point it out."

Charles turned his eyes into blue ice.

"So," whispered Andrew, swallowing hard, "what exactly do you want me to do?"

"Find a way to sneak into Community Meeting Room *B*."

Andrew wheezed in panic. "That's impossible."

"Don't worry. I have an idea."

"What is it?"

"Two words: Sierra Russell."

37

"Ever wonder if this could reek any worse?" said Akimi. "Because it couldn't."

"Yo, none of us pulled a Clunker Card," groused Miguel. "That means somebody on Charles's team did it."

"Akimi and Miguel are right, Kyle," said Sierra. "This really isn't fair."

"I know," was all Kyle could say. "But it's like in Mr Lemoncello's Family Frenzy, where one player pulls the Orthodontist card and *everybody* has to move back seven spaces to buy their kids braces."

Kyle and his teammates were back in Community Meeting Room B. They'd been staring at the clue board, wondering what a wailing blackbird had to do with Willy Wonka and the Ten Commandments – not to mention that long list of books and all the statues – when the voice in the ceiling made its announcement about the Dewey decimal doors being locked for fourteen hours.

"Well, Mr Lemoncello better have a *good* reason," said Akimi.

"Oh, I do," said Mr Lemoncello.

His face appeared on one of the meeting room walls, which was really a giant plasma-screen video monitor.

"Team Kyle is not being penalized for Team Charles's blunder," he said. "Far from it. In fact, you are being rewarded."

Akimi arched her eyebrows in disbelief. "Really? How?"

"The other team's penalty gives you a wrinkle in time."

"A wrinkle in time?" said Kyle. "Is that a clue?"

"No. It's a book. And sometimes, Kyle, a book is just a book. But thanks to the Clunker Card, you have the gift of wrinkled time to seek clues *outside* the ten Dewey decimal rooms. Speaking of *Time*, a magazine available in our periodicals section, it's dinnertime!"

"So the game is basically suspended until ten o'clock tomorrow?" said Kyle.

"Well, Kyle, that's up to you. You can use this time as a bonus, to think, read and explore. Or you can run upstairs and play video games all night long. The choice is yours."

"We want to win *this* game," said Kyle. His teammates nodded in agreement.

"Wondermous!" said Mr Lemoncello. "Keep working the puzzle but try to avoid Mrs Basil E. Frankweiler's files.

They're all mixed up. And before you turn in this evening, you might want to spend some time curled up with a good book."

"Um, they just said the book rooms are locked," said Akimi.

"The nice lady in the ceiling was only talking about the ten Dewey decimal rooms. There is plenty of first-class fiction in the Rotunda Reading Room. Dr Zinchenko has even selected seven books specifically for our seven remaining contestants. After dinner, you'll find those books on her desk."

When he said that, Mr Lemoncello started winking.

"I think you'll find the books to be very *enlightening*. Inspirational, even."

And then he winked some more.

"And now, I must return to my side of the mountain. See you in the morning, children! I have great expectations for you all!"

Mr Lemoncello's image disappeared from the wall.

"OK," said Akimi, "from the way Mr Lemoncello was just winking, either somebody kicked a bucket of sand in his face or our recommended reading list is another clue."

On the other side of the rotunda, Charles huddled with Andrew in Meeting Room A.

"I don't trust Haley," he said.

"Why not?"

Charles placed his hand on Andrew's shoulder. "Well, my friend, I'm not sure if I should tell you this, but Haley told me she didn't think you were 'handsome enough' to appear in Mr Lemoncello's holiday commercials with us when we win."

"Because of my glasses?"

Charles bit his lip. Nodded. "Of course, I totally disagree."

"I see," said Andrew, his ears burning bright red. "Then she doesn't get to see what we found in that *Anne of Green Gables* book."

"Very well, Andrew. If that's how you want to play it."

"You bet I do."

"Fine. Let's go see what's for dinner. I'm starving."

When Charles and Andrew entered the cafe, the Keeley team was already inside, filling their trays.

"Hey, way to go, Charles!" joked Miguel Fernandez. "You guys pulled a Clunker Card?"

"Indeed we did. However, not even that bit of bad luck can derail our juggernaut!"

"Huh?" said Akimi.

"He means we're still gonna win!" said Andrew.

Charles and Andrew crossed to the far side of the room to join Haley, who was sitting in a corner.

"You guys find any clues this afternoon?" she asked.

"Sadly, no," said Charles.

"All we found was that door-locking penalty," said Andrew, who could lie almost as well as Charles.

"How about you, Haley?" Charles asked. "Find any-thing interesting?"

"Nope. Nada." Then she yawned and finished her dinner. "I think I'll head upstairs and sack out."

"Really? It's only eight-forty-eight."

"I know. But I'm totally pooped." She yawned again. "Plus, I want to be up bright and early, before the Dewey decimal doors reopen. We have more clues to find. See you guys tomorrow. Unless we have more team business to discuss?"

"No. Nothing."

She walked out of the cafe.

38

"Very interesting," said Akimi, looking through the cafe's glass walls and into the Rotunda Reading Room.

"What?" said Miguel.

"I think Clarence just dropped off our books."

Kyle pushed back from the table. He could see the shadowy figure of the bulky security guard slinking away from the round desk at the centre of the rotunda. He left behind a stack of books.

"Come on," he said. "Let's go see what sort of 'inspirational' reading Dr Zinchenko has selected for us."

"What about those guys?" said Miguel, gesturing towards the table where Charles and Andrew were finishing their desserts.

Kyle was torn.

On one hand, he didn't want to give away the bonus his team had received thanks to the other team's penalty.

On the other hand, he didn't want people saying he and his friends won because Mr Lemoncello had tossed them an extra clue.

He came up with a compromise.

"Hey, Charles? Andrew? We're all going to go grab some books to read to kill time till tomorrow morning. You two might want to do the same thing."

"No thanks." Charles stood up. "We pretty much have this thing figured out. In fact, I think Mr Lemoncello steered us towards the Clunker Card so we wouldn't win too easily. I mean, how would it look if we escaped from his library in less than twenty-four hours?"

"Bad," said Andrew. "Real bad."

"Indeed," said Charles. "In fact, I suspect nobody would buy Lemoncello games any more if we showed them how consistently easy they are to win. Anyway, we're going upstairs so I can give Andrew a tour of my private suite. Would any of you care to join us?"

"No thanks," said Akimi.

"Suit yourself. Oh, by the way, Mr Lemoncello has a real video game console upstairs."

Kyle felt his mouth going dry.

"It's top-of-the-line equipment. And it plays real games. Not just educational stuff. Care to join us, Keeley?"

"Um . . ."

"We're going to play Squirrel Squad Six. The new edition. According to the game box, it won't be released to the general public until early December."

Kyle felt sweat beading on his forehead. His palms were moist. His fingers were twitching, itching to thumb-toggle a joystick.

But finally, after the inside of his mouth had turned to sandpaper, he said, "No thanks, Charles. We're just gonna, you know, read."

After Charles and Andrew headed up to the second floor to play what was probably the most awesome version ever of Mr Lemoncello's most awesome video game ever (if Charles Chiltington was actually telling the truth), Kyle and his teammates hurried out to see what books were waiting for them on the librarian's table.

They found seven different versions of the same book: *The Complete Sherlock Holmes*. One was a leather-bound limited edition; another was a tattered paperback; three were hardcovers with different illustrations on their fronts; one was a bigger kind of paperback with lots of scholarly essays; and the seventh was an e-reader with only the one title loaded on to it.

"I think Mr Lemoncello wants us to start a book club," said Sierra.

"What do you mean?" asked Kyle.

"You know – we all read the same book and then get together later to discuss it and share our opinions."

"It's fun," said Miguel. "We have a book group at school."

"Are you in it?" asked Sierra.

"Yeah. Maybe you'd like to join us sometime?"

"I would. Thank you, Miguel."

Akimi cleared her throat. "Now what?" she said to Kyle.

Kyle shrugged. "Like I told Charles. We read."

Everybody grabbed a copy of the Sherlock Holmes book.

Nobody went for the e-reader.

Upstairs on the second floor, Haley tiptoed around the Lemoncello-abilia Room.

When she had visited the mini-museum earlier, she hadn't really looked around. Now she hoped to find another book from the "memorable reads" display, a Little Golden Book called *Baby's Mother Goose: Pat-a-Cake,* which could've been something Mr Lemoncello read (or had read to him) when he was a very young boy.

Haley made her way past the orderly stacks of boxes through a doorway and into what looked like a re-creation of Mr Lemoncello's childhood bedroom – a cramped space crammed with two bunk beds that he had shared with his three brothers. Next to one of the lower bunks was a bookcase made out of plastic milk crates.

There it was, filed away with maybe three dozen other skinny, hardboard-covered picture books.

Haley pried open the cover.

Out plopped a four-by-four art card:

 **+ ED**

She quickly folded it in half and stuffed it inside her sneaker with her "BANDITS" clue.

Because now she was pretty certain that "bandits" had, at one time or another, "crawled in" to this building back when it was a bank.

The silhouette of Indiana didn't represent the Indianapolis 500 like Charles had insisted.

It stood for "IN", the official post office abbreviation for the Hoosier State.

First thing in the morning, when the doors reopened, she needed to search through the Dewey decimal rooms to find a clue that would tell her exactly how and where the bandits had crawled in.

A tunnel? An air vent? A secret passageway on the ground, first or second floor between the old bank and the office building behind it?

There was only one thing Haley was certain of: they hadn't crawled in through a book return slot.

39

Everyone in the reading room was quietly lost in the adventures of Sherlock Holmes.

Kyle had just finished a pretty cool story called "A Scandal in Bohemia", about a king who was going to get married to a royal heiress with maybe six names. But the king was being blackmailed by an old girlfriend, an opera singer from New Jersey named Irene Adler.

Something Sherlock Holmes said to Dr Watson early in the story really stuck with Kyle: "You see, but you do not observe."

Kyle figured that was why Mr Lemoncello wanted them all to take a break from chasing clues and read these classic mysteries. Not to find new clues but to become better puzzle solvers. Had they been seeing things without really observing them? Probably.

Reading the story was also kind of fun. Kyle could

totally see Holmes's apartment at 221b Baker Street and the snooty king and the horse-drawn carriages on the foggy London streets and the disguises Holmes wore and the smoke bomb Dr Watson tossed through a window and everybody on the street screaming, "Fire!"

It was like he was watching a 3-D IMAX movie in his head. Kyle couldn't wait to start the second story in the book, "The Adventure of the Red-Headed League."

"How's it going?" whispered Akimi.

"This book is pretty cool. This Sir Arthur Conan Doyle guy knows how to keep his readers hooked."

"His characters leap off the pages," said Sierra.

"Yeah," said Miguel. "I dig the 'consulting detective'."

"Huh?" said Kyle.

"That's what Holmes calls himself sometimes."

"Oh. I've only read one story so far and . . ."

Suddenly, something seemed odd to Kyle.

"Hey—how come Conan Doyle isn't one of those statues up there?"

"What do you mean?" said Akimi.

"He's a famous author, right? How come they're projecting a statue of a modern writer like Pseudonymous Bosch but not the author who created a classic like Sherlock Holmes?"

"Good question, bro," said Miguel.

"I need to *consult* with my brother Curtis."

"How come?"

"Curtis has read more books than anyone I know,

except maybe Sierra. He scored an 808 on his SAT Subject Test in Literature."

"Uh, Kyle?" said Akimi. "I think the top score for any SAT test is 800."

"Yep. Then Curtis took it. They had to raise it."

"So maybe he can help us figure out what's up with all the statues," said Miguel.

"Exactly. Why these ten? Why not ten other writers?"

"Why not the same ten Bridgette Wadge had for her Extreme Challenge?" added Sierra.

Kyle looked around the room.

"Mrs Tobin? Hello? Mrs Tobin?"

The hazy holographic image of the 1960s librarian flickered into view.

"How may I help you, KYLE?"

"I'd like to talk to an expert."

"And whom do you wish to speak to?"

"Mr Curtis Keeley."

"Your brother?"

"And an SAT-certified expert on the subject of literature and authors and other literary-type junk."

Suddenly, the hologram vanished and Dr Zinchenko's voice came over the ceiling speakers.

"This is a rather irregular request, Mr Keeley."

"Hey," said Akimi, "this whole game is rather irregular, don't ya think?"

"We just need some more data," said Kyle. "Because,

like Sherlock says to Dr Watson, 'it is a capital mistake to theorize before one has data.'"

"I take it you're enjoying your book?" said the librarian.

Kyle gave the closest security camera a big thumbs-up. "Boo-yeah. Can't wait to see what's up with that league of redheaded gentlemen."

"Ah, yes," said Dr Zinchenko. "A fascinating story. I recently reread it myself. Very well, Kyle. We will contact your brother to determine if he does indeed qualify as a literary expert. It may take a while."

"No rush," said Kyle. "I've got a good book."

Kyle was busy helping Holmes figure out that the Red-Headed League was just a clever ploy pulled by some robbers to get a red-haired pawnbroker to leave his shop long enough for them to dig a tunnel from his basement to the bank next door when the librarian's voice jolted him out of London and brought him home to Ohio.

"My apologies for the interruption."

Akimi, Miguel and Sierra closed their books, too. It was eleven-fifteen. Everyone had sleepy, dreamy looks in their eyes because they'd been kind of drifting off in their comfy reading chairs.

"What's up?" said Kyle.

"We have arranged for your expert consultation with Mr Curtis Keeley."

"Awesome! How do we do it?"

"You and your expert may have a five-minute video chat on my computer terminal, which is located behind the main desk."

Kyle hurried over to the round desk in the centre of the room. His three teammates hurried right behind him.

"Your consultation begins . . . now."

And there was Curtis. Sitting at his computer in his bedroom.

"Hey, Curtis!"

"Hi, Kyle. How's it going in there?"

"Great."

Kyle's oldest brother, Mike, popped into the doorway behind Curtis.

"Ky-le, Ky-le," Mike chanted. "Whoo-hoo!"

Kyle had never had his own cheerleader before.

"We need you to give us one hundred and ten percent in there, li'l brother!" Mike squinted at the screen over Curtis's shoulder. "Who are those other guys?"

"My teammates, Miguel, Sierra and you know Akimi."

"You guys are a team? Smart move. Even I can't win football games without help from ten other guys."

"Um, Mike?" said Kyle. "Curtis and I only have five minutes to chat."

"Cool. I'm outta here. Win, baby, win!"

Mike back-pedalled out of the bedroom, making double fist pumps the whole way.

"You have four minutes remaining," advised Dr Zinchenko.

"OK, Curtis, here's my question. What do these authors have in common?"

Kyle rattled off the list of the statues in order.

And Curtis stared blankly into his computer cam.

For a real long time.

Then he shook his head. "I'm sorry, Kyle. I have no earthly idea."

40

"Really?" Kyle was astonished. "You've got nothing?"

"Well," said Curtis, "the only connection I can see is Thomas Wolfe wrote *Look Homeward, Angel* and Lewis Carroll wrote *Through the Looking-Glass*. Both titles have the word 'look' in them. But the two books are otherwise completely different. The two authors as well."

Kyle and his whole team stood in stunned silence.

Until Sierra started jumping up and down.

"Of course!" she shouted.

"Your time is up," announced Dr Zinchenko.

"Um, OK," Kyle said to the computer screen. "Thanks, Curtis. That was, uh, really helpful."

"It was!" said Sierra, daintily clapping her hands together like a very polite seal. The computer screen faded to black.

"What's up?" asked Miguel.

"I think I know how to crack the statue code."

"There's a code?" said Akimi. "Who knew?"

"It'll take time," said Sierra. "And I need a computer."

"OK . . ." said Kyle, who was sort of shocked to see Sierra so completely jazzed. "We'll be in our meeting room, putting together a list of new Dewey decimal numbers from the Bibliomania cards so we're ready to hit the ground running when the doors reopen at ten tomorrow morning."

While Sierra settled in at a desktop computer pad, the rest of the team returned to the Bibliomania board game.

"We should just start flipping over cards and putting together a list of call numbers," Kyle suggested.

"Sounds like a plan," said Akimi.

She plucked a purple card out of the pile.

Lose a Turn was all that was printed on the other side.

"Try a different colour," urged Miguel.

Akimi flipped up a blue card.

Take an Extra Turn was printed on it. So Akimi flipped over all the other blue cards while Miguel flipped over all the purples.

The purple cards all said **Lose a Turn**. The blue ones all said **Take an Extra Turn**.

Kyle had been checking out the red and maroon piles.

"The reds all say 'Pick a Yellow Card'," he reported. "The maroons say 'Grab a Green'."

"The greys do the same thing," said Miguel. "Only they say 'Pick a Pink'. The tan cards say 'Go Grab an Orange'."

"So that leaves the colours we've already played." Kyle flipped over a yellow card. "'In the square root of 48,629.20271209 . . .'"

"What the . . . ?" said Akimi.

"Hang on," said Miguel. "There's a calculator app in this desktop computer."

Kyle read the rest of the card: ". . . 'find half of 4-40-30'."

"Well, that's 2-20-15, again," said Akimi.

"And the square root of forty-eight thousand whatever is 220.5203," said Miguel. "The King James Bible we already found."

Akimi flipped through the rest of the yellow cards. "Same with these. They all send us into the Religion section to find that Bible verse."

"Ditto with the greens," reported Miguel. "All clues leading to *Bird Songs, Warbles and Whistles*."

"And the pinks all lead back to 027.4," said Kyle. "I guess they really wanted to make sure we found *Get to Know Your Local Library*."

"Which leaves the wild cards," said Akimi. She examined the orange deck. "Find a rhyme for 'cart and paperbacks', 'smart and zodiacs', 'tart and potato sacks'."

"The Art and Artifacts Room," said Miguel with a sigh.

"Where," Akimi continued, "we need to find a rhyme for 'Randy', 'Sandy' or 'Brandi'."

213

"The Willy Wonka candy," said Miguel.

"So," said Kyle, "I'm guessing the Bibliomania game was only supposed to help us find the four clues we've already found."

"But we need to know more numbers," said Miguel. "Because a library should be a know-place for know-bodies."

When Miguel made his pun, Kyle and Akimi both groaned.

But then Kyle thought of something: "This is why Mr Lemoncello called our time-out a bonus. He knew we'd need a ton of time to find a new source of numbers."

Just then Sierra burst into the meeting room.

"You guys! I found a whole bunch of new numbers!"

"What?" said Kyle, Akimi and Miguel. "Where?"

"Up on the ceiling!"

41

"You need to look up at the Wonder Dome," said Sierra.

"Huh?" said Kyle.

Sierra and her whole team were standing together outside the door to Community Meeting Room B. She hadn't been this happy or excited in a long time.

"Um, Sierra?" said Akimi. "Why exactly are you suggesting we all give ourselves a crick in the neck by staring at the ceiling?"

"OK. This is a game some of us play online called What's the Connection? I put up a list of authors and you have to figure out how they're linked by the titles of their books."

"Whoa," said Akimi, sort of sarcastically. "Sounds like fun."

"It is. But believe me, it's not easy."

"What'd you figure out?" asked Miguel.

"Well, like Curtis said, Thomas Wolfe wrote *Look Homeward, Angel* and Lewis Carroll wrote *Through the Looking-Glass*. That got me thinking. And running computer searches. Stephen Sondheim wrote a book called *Look, I Made a Hat*. Maya Angelou wrote *Even the Stars Look Lonesome* and Pseudonymous Bosch wrote *This Isn't What It Looks Like*."

"They all have 'look' in the title," said Kyle.

"What about the other five authors?" asked Akimi. "Did they write 'look' books, too?"

"No, they're up there for a different word."

"Huh?"

"Booker T. Washington wrote *Up from Slavery* and Shel Silverstein wrote *Falling Up*."

"And Dr Seuss?" said Kyle.

"*Great Day for Up*. George Orwell did *Coming Up for Air* and Todd Strasser has a book called *If I Grow Up*."

"So the ten statues give us two words," said Miguel.

"Yep. 'Look' and 'up.' So I did. I looked up. At the Wonder Dome. There! Did you see it? That string of numbers that just drifted across the two hundreds screen under the Star of David?"

"220.5203," said Miguel.

Akimi knuckle-punched Kyle in the arm. "This is just like that bonus code thingie you showed me on the school bus!"

"Of course," said Kyle. "This is a Lemoncello game.

216

He always hides secret codes in screwy places. Way to go, Sierra!"

"Thanks," said Sierra, realizing how much more fun it was to play this kind of game with real friends instead of virtual ones on the internet.

"But we already found that same two hundreds number playing Bibliomania," said Miguel.

"True," said Kyle. "Check out the sections for numbers the cards wouldn't give us."

Everybody craned their necks and focused on the graphics swimming across the ten panels overhead.

"Here comes another one!" said Sierra. "In the six hundreds. Right underneath the floating stethoscope."

"Got it!" said Kyle. "624.193."

"Whoo-hoo!" said Akimi.

"Sierra, you're my new hero," said Kyle. "You saved the day."

Sierra blushed. "Thanks."

"The spinner," said Akimi.

"Huh?" said Miguel.

"That was another clue. The Bibliomania game was pointing us to the ceiling, too. Because in Dewey decimal mode, the Wonder Dome looks like a giant 3-D version of the board game's spinner."

"Awesome, Sierra," said Miguel. "Absolutely awesome."

* * *

217

Sierra and her teammates stared up at the ceiling for over an hour. At 12:30, they finally lay down on the floor so they wouldn't cramp their neck muscles.

Because every fifteen minutes, the animated ceiling looped through call numbers for every Dewey decimal room in the library.

Except one.

And then the sequence repeated itself.

"How come there's no three hundreds number?" said Miguel.

"Probably because that's the one book we really, really, *really* need," said Kyle.

"That Lemoncello," said Akimi. "What a comedian."

42

Peering over the railing on the second-floor balcony at close to 2 a.m., Andrew Peckleman saw Sierra Russell sitting all alone in the Rotunda Reading Room.

Andrew had spent the night on the second floor losing video games to Charles.

And being reminded about how much he needed to break into Community Meeting Room B to "borrow" any clues Kyle Keeley's team had gathered, to pay Charles back for wasting so much of "the team's time" on the *Anne of Green Gables* clue due to his "foolish fear" of heights.

Andrew had promised Charles he'd do whatever it took.

"If anyone on Team Keeley is going to help us break into their headquarters," Charles had said, "it will be the shy girl who is constantly reading. Have you noticed what Sierra Russell uses for a bookmark?"

"No," Andrew had honestly answered.

"Her library card, which of course doubles as a key card for Meeting Room B. Find a way to borrow it."

"Isn't that illegal?"

"Of course not. This is a library. People borrow books, don't they?"

"Well, yeah . . ."

"Did I mention that I have three thousand Facebook friends? Two thousand Twitter followers? Each and every one of them will hear what a weenie and wimp you are if you don't do this thing to guarantee that our team wins."

So Andrew made his way down to the ground floor.

Sierra, as usual, was reading a book.

As he moved closer, Andrew saw a flash of white.

Charles was right. Sierra was using her shiny white library card to mark her place in the book's pages.

He made his way to the cluster of overstuffed reading chairs.

"Good book?"

His voice startled her.

"Oh. Hello. Yes."

"Mind if I join you?" He slid into a crinkly leather seat opposite Sierra. "So, um, what're you reading?"

"*Charlie and the Great Glass Elevator* by Roald Dahl."

"Oh, yeah. I've heard about that book. Where's the rest of your team?"

"They went to bed. Want to get up bright and early. Before the doors on the first floor open again."

"Yeah. Haley and Charles conked out, too. Guess it's just us bookworms, huh?"

"Well, it is kind of late," said Sierra. "I'm going to go upstairs and . . ."

"May I take a look?"

"Hmmm?"

"At your book. I've never actually read it. I just tell people I have."

"Oh. Sure." Sierra handed it to him.

"Thank you."

Andrew flipped through the pages until he found the spot where Sierra had tucked in her library card. "Wouldn't it be cool if this library had a flying elevator like in that Willy Wonka movie? Especially if you could use it to crash through the roof like Charlie and Wonka did. That'd be a pretty cool way to escape from the library, huh?"

"Yeah. I guess."

That was when Andrew made the switch. He slipped his library card into Sierra's book and palmed hers.

Charles would be so proud of him!

"So," he said, closing the book, "did you ever read *The Elevator Family*?"

"No. I don't think so."

"It's all about this family that lives in the elevator of a San Francisco hotel. And let's just say, the book has its ups and its downs!"

Andrew laughed hysterically, because it was one of the

funniest jokes he knew. Sierra sort of chuckled. He handed back her book.

Overhead, the Wonder Dome dissolved out of its Dewey decimal mode and, with a swirl of colours, became a bright green bedroom with a pair of red-framed windows looking out on a blue night sky with a full moon and a blanket of twinkling stars. In the great green room, there was a telephone, and a red balloon, and a picture of a cow jumping over the moon.

The ceiling had become the bunny's bedroom from *Goodnight Moon*.

A quiet old lady bunny in a frumpy blue dress hopped into the Rotunda Reading Room. Two tiny cats followed her.

"Great," said Andrew. "Another stupid hologram."

"I think she's cute," said Sierra.

"Hush," said the bunny. "Goodnight clocks and goodnight socks. Goodnight, Sierra."

"Goodnight, Bunny." Sierra took her book and headed upstairs.

"Goodnight, Andrew," said the bunny.

"Right."

He pocketed the purloined library card. He couldn't do anything with it right away. Not while the holographic bunny's handlers were watching on the spy cameras.

But first thing in the morning . . .

"Goodnight old bunny saying hush," he called out.

And then, under his breath, he muttered, "In the morning, our competition we're gonna crush."

43

Up bright and early the next morning, Kyle made his way across the Rotunda Reading Room.

It was eight-fifteen. The Dewey decimal doors would open in one hour and forty-five minutes. The game would be over in less than four hours.

Kyle was totally pumped.

Sierra Russell, on the other hand, was sitting in a comfy chair reading a book.

"Hey," said Kyle.

"Hi," said Sierra, stifling a small yawn.

"Did you stay up all night reading?"

"No. I went upstairs around two. But there was a new stack of books on the librarian's desk when I came down."

"Oh, really? What'd you find?"

"Five copies of this."

She showed Kyle her book. It was *The Eleventh Hour: A Curious Mystery.*

"It's a rhyming picture book about Horace the Elephant's eleventh birthday party and the search to find out who ran off with all the food. There are hidden messages and cryptic codes all over the pages."

"Why's it called *The Eleventh Hour?*"

"The birthday feast was supposed to take place at eleven a.m. But since somebody stole all the food . . ."

Kyle laughed. "Eleven a.m."

"What?"

"The eleventh hour! The last possible moment." Kyle nudged his head up at the Wonder Dome. "How much do you want to bet that at eleven o'clock, on the dot, the clue we need most of all will pop up in the three hundreds section?"

Sierra smiled. "So this new book is a clue about our clue?"

"That's my guess. Did you eat breakfast?"

"Not yet."

"Well, what are you waiting for?" said Miguel as he strode into the room. "Today's the big day. We're gonna need our energy for the final sprint."

"He's right," said Akimi, climbing down the spiral staircase. "The doors open in less than two hours. Then we only have two more hours to figure everything out."

"But," said Kyle to his other teammates, "Sierra just figured out when we'll get the big three hundreds clue."

He gestured towards the picture book. "At the last possible minute."

"What?" said Akimi. "Eleven-fifty-nine?"

"Close. Eleven o'clock."

"Awesome," said Miguel. "It must be a very good clue."

Kyle and his team went into the cafe, where they found Haley Daley seated at a table, eating half a grapefruit and staring blankly through the glass walls into the rotunda.

"Hey, Haley," said Kyle. "How's it going?"

"Not bad. You?"

"Good. Win or lose, we're having a blast."

"We're the fun bunch," said Akimi.

"You guys really get along, huh?"

"Oh, yes," said Sierra. "I haven't had this much fun since I was six."

"Seriously?"

"What's the matter, Haley?" said Akimi. "Life not so good on Team Charles?"

"It's OK, I guess. I mean, we've pulled together some good clues and all . . ."

"Well," said Miguel, "if you ever want to switch sides, we're always looking for new members."

"Can I do that? Just switch sides? Even though I know everything about what Team Charles did all day yesterday?"

"I think so," said Kyle. "I mean, there was nothing in the rules about teams."

"Huh," said Haley. "And Andrew's teamed up with you guys, too?"

"No," said Kyle.

Haley nodded towards the wall of windows behind Kyle. "Then why'd he just swipe his library card and go into your meeting room?"

44

Zipping across the slick marble floor, Kyle and his team, trailed by Haley, practically slid into Community Meeting Room B.

Where Andrew Peckleman stood with a notepad jotting down everything that was written on the whiteboard walls.

"Hey!" shouted Akimi. "That's cheating!"

Andrew spun around.

His eyes were the size of tennis balls behind his goggle glasses.

"Uh, uh, uh," he sputtered. "You guys left the door open!"

"No we did not," said Kyle extremely calmly, especially considering how much he wanted to throttle Peckleman. "It locks automatically; I checked."

"And I double-checked the door before we went to bed," said Miguel.

Kyle was surprised to hear it. "You did?"

"You bet, bro. It's what teammates do."

They knocked knuckles.

"Well, you don't have anything but a stupid list of stupid books and stupid authors and a stupid Bible verse . . ."

"A verse which," boomed Mr Lemoncello, whose face had just appeared on the video-screen wall, "you would do well to memorize, Mr Peckleman. 'Thou shalt not steal.' "

Mr Lemoncello was dressed in a curled white wig and a long black robe. He looked like a judge in England. He slammed down a rubber gavel on his desk. It made a noise like a whoopee cushion.

"Will everyone kindly join me in the Rotunda Reading Room? At once."

Everybody shuffled out of the meeting room and into the rotunda. They were shocked to see that Mr Lemoncello himself was seated behind the librarian's desk at the centre of the circular room. This was no hologram. This was the real deal.

Charles, all smiles, made a grand entrance, slowly descending one of the spiral staircases.

"Good morning, everybody," he called out cheerfully. "What's all the excitement? Did I miss something?"

"Just your man Andrew trying to cheat," said Miguel.

"What? Oh, good morning, Mr Lemoncello. I didn't expect to find you here, inside the library. Isn't today your birthday, sir?"

"Yes, Charles. And there's no place I'd rather be on my

big day than inside a library, surrounded by books. Unless, of course, I could be on a bridge to Terabithia."

"Well, sir, I must say, you're certainly looking fit and trim. Have you been working out?"

"No, Charles, today I will be working *in*."

"I beg your pardon?"

"Today I will be working here, inside the library, supervising the final hours of this competition."

"Oh, I don't think it will take *hours,* sir," said Charles. "Not to brag, but I suspect some of us will be going home very soon."

"You are correct. For instance, Mr Peckleman. He will be leaving right now."

"What?" whined Peckleman. "Why?"

"Because you cheated. You tried to steal the other team's hard-earned information."

Peckleman's eyes darted back and forth. "It wasn't my fault. It was Charles's idea." He whipped up his arm and waggled his finger. "Charles told me to do it. He *made* me do it!"

"Mr Peckleman, please approach the bench, which, in this instance, is actually a desk. Let me see the library card you used to gain access to Community Meeting Room B."

Somewhat reluctantly, Andrew handed it over.

"Is your name Sierra Russell?"

"No, sir," Andrew said to his shoes.

"He stole my card?" said Sierra. She opened her latest book and pulled out the library card bookmark.

"Whose card do you have, Sierra?" asked Charles.

"Andrew Peckleman's."

"Aha," said Charles. "He pulled the old switcheroo, eh?"

"Because you told me to!" said Peckleman.

"Really?" Charles said, sniggering. "How dare you make such a scandalous accusation? Do you have any proof?"

"I don't need any stupid proof. You bullied me into stealing Sierra's card!"

Mr Lemoncello banged his gavel again. "And thus ends the story of Andrew and the terrible, horrible, no good, very bad day. Mrs Bunny?"

A hologram of the old lady bunny from *Goodnight Moon* hopped on top of the librarian's desk.

"Goodnight, Andrew," said the bunny. "Your time with us is all through."

Clarence and Clement, the security guards, appeared and escorted Peckleman out of the building.

"Sir?" said Sierra. "Would you like Andrew's library card for the discard pile?"

"No, thank you. That card is now property of Team Kyle."

Haley Daley raised her hand.

"Yes, Haley?"

Kyle saw her shoot a withering glance at Charles.

"How may I help you, dear?" asked Mr Lemoncello.

"Well, sir, if it's OK with you, I'd like to switch sides. I want to join Kyle Keeley's team."

45

"*Zap!*" said Mr Lemoncello, waving his arms like a magician. "*Zip!* You're now on Kyle Keeley's team!"

"Haley?" said Charles. "How can you desert me?"

"The same way you just deserted Andrew."

"Um, do we get *her* library card, too?" asked Kyle.

"Indeed you do. Plus any and all information she chooses to share with you. And so, Charles, I ask you: Would *you* like to quit your team and join Kyle's?"

"Excuse me?"

"You know, all for one and one for all?"

"Sir, with all due respect, that may have worked for those three musketeers in a trumped-up work of fiction, but I'm sorry, that is not how things work in the real world. Out here, it's every man for himself. What good is a prize if everyone wins it?"

"I see. But Haley knows all the clues you've collected."

"True, sir. But I doubt she realizes what any of them mean."

Kyle could see Mr Lemoncello's nose twitch when Charles said that. And it wasn't a happy-bunny kind of twitch, either.

"It was a joke, sir." Charles must've seen the nose twitch, too.

"Oh. I see. Like the one about the boy named Charles. Hilarious. Remind me to tell it to you sometime. Anyway, be that as it may, I insist that you be given a few extra clues to compensate for the fact that all your teammates are either being kicked out of the game or abandoning your ship." Mr Lemoncello reached under the desk and pulled out a white envelope. "This, Charles, is for your eyes only."

Charles stepped forward and took the envelope.

"Thank you, sir. That is very generous."

"I know. You may also ask me one question. But please, don't waste your question asking me, 'Where is the alternate exit?' because I do not know."

"You don't know?" Kyle said it before Charles could.

"Haven't a clue. This entire game was designed by my head librarian, Dr Yanina Zinchenko, as my birthday present."

"But," said Akimi, "you could just ask Dr Zinchenko how to get out, right?"

"Akimi Hughes? Are you one of those people who read the last chapter of a book first to see how it ends?"

"No, but . . ."

"Good. It's much more fun when the ending is a surprise. Dr Zinchenko is the only one who knows how and where to exit this building without setting off all sorts of fire alarms. Any clues I personally delivered during the course of this game were completely scripted for me by Dr Z."

"OK," said Charles, "here's my question . . ."

Mr Lemoncello raised a hand. "Before you ask it, be advised: Your opponents will also hear my answer."

"Fine. Why is the book on the bedside table in your private suite *From the Mixed-Up Files of Mrs Basil E. Frankweiler* by E. L. Konigsburg?"

"Because when I was your age, Mrs Tobin, my local librarian, gave it to me."

Miguel raised his hand.

"Yes, Miguel?"

"Can we have one bonus question, too?" he asked politely.

"No," said Mr Lemoncello. "However, I will give you one bonus answer, which Charles, of course, will also hear. Your bonus answer is 'lodgepole, loblolly and Rocky Mountain white.'"

"What are three different kinds of pine trees?" said Charles, just to show off – and to let Kyle's team know their bonus answer didn't give them any kind of advantage.

"I am told that is correct," said Mr Lemoncello, touching his ear.

He reached under the desk again and this time pulled up a three-foot-tall hourglass, a giant version of the red plastic timers that came as standard equipment in a lot of his games.

He turned it over.

"It's the jumbo, three-hour size," he said as the sand started trickling down. "Because it is now nine o'clock and you have only three more hours to find your way out of the library. Good luck. And may the best team – or, in Charles's case, the best solo effort – win!"

46

"Let's see what kind of *real* bonus clues Mr Lemoncello is serving up today," Charles said to his empty conference room.

He really didn't mind flying solo. It meant he wouldn't have to share his prize when he won it.

Winner won all.

Losers lost all.

That was just the way the world rolled.

And Charles knew he would win.

After all, he was a Chiltington. They never lost.

Even if he had wasted his question about the *Mixed-Up Files* book. Turned out that Mr Lemoncello was just a sentimental sap like Kyle Keeley. The book was there because his beloved librarian gave it to the old fool when he was the same age as all the library lock-in contestants. Boo-hoo. Big whoop.

And what was all that nonsense about pine trees?
Preposterous.

Unclasping the sealed envelope, Charles found two silhouette cards. Each of them was numbered, in case Charles couldn't figure out which books they would've been hidden in.

#8

Babied? Charles wondered. *No. Crawled!*
He examined the second free card.

#12

Three dinners? Three couples? A restaurant?
This one was difficult.

Charles decided to put the two new pieces into the puzzle, to see if their meanings would become clearer:

Charles was missing only one clue, but he had everything else.

"You can walk out the way BLANK crawled in in passed restaurant."

No. That didn't make sense.

In fact, all he was really certain about were the first two lines: "You can walk out the way."

The way what? Past the restaurant? The Book Nook Cafe?

And what about the image of the football player?

It came from the Johnny Unitas book. Maybe Johnny Unitas, who had played football back when Mr Lemoncello was Charles's age, had owned a restaurant? Perhaps a popular national chain?

If so, there might've been one in Alexandriaville. Maybe right here in the old Gold Leaf Bank building.

Could the last bit be "In Johnny Unitas's Restaurant"?

Or what if Andrew Peckleman had been right all along and it was the NINETEEN that was the clue from the football player card? That would make the final line "In nineteen . . ." WHAT? *Diners? Couples?*

No.

Anniversaries!

The three couples in the bonus clue were obviously celebrating their anniversaries!

Nineteen anniversaries? Was today the nineteenth anniversary of some major event in Alexandriaville?

Charles shook his head. He knew the phrase would make sense only *after* he had completed the third line, the only one that still had a blank in it: "BLANK, CRAWLED, INN."

What if the missing image is an eyeball? Then the third line could be "I crawled *in.*"

Hang on, Charles thought. The one book in the Staff Picks display case nobody had found yet was *True Crime Ohio: The Buckeye State's Most Notorious Brigands, Burglars and Bandits* by Clare Taylor-Winters. The last image was going to be a criminal of some sort.

That one, single missing book might tell Charles who had crawled into the bank and, more importantly, *where* they had crawled in. Was this the nineteenth anniversary of a famous bank robbery?

Charles realized he needed help.

It was time to use his Ask an Expert.

That made him laugh.

Because Charles knew the top library expert in all of America, maybe the world. Someone much more important than Dr Yanina Zinchenko.

Kyle Keeley and the rest of that bunch didn't stand a chance.

47

Eager to find out all he could in the final minutes before the Dewey decimal doors reopened on the first floor, Kyle listened as Haley Daley detailed everything she had learned on Team Charles.

Meanwhile, Akimi added Andrew's and Haley's library cards to the list on the whiteboards in Community Meeting Room B.

"We were piecing together a picture puzzle," said Haley. "It was like a memory match game, or that old TV show *Concentration*."

"We played one of those, too," said Miguel. "A rebus."

"Right. So far, I'm pretty sure it says something like 'You walk out the way bandits crawled in'."

"'Thou shalt not steal'," said Kyle, tapping the Bible verse they had found in the 200s room. "That points to bandits, too."

240

"And the blackbird," said Sierra. "It wailed like a police siren."

"Chasing bandits!"

"Hang on," said Miguel. "What about Willy Wonka? Were there criminals in the chocolate factory?"

"No," said Sierra.

"And what about all this?" said Akimi, pointing at the list of library cards. "I added the new cards but it still doesn't make much sense."

BOOKS/AUTHORS ON THE BACKS OF LIBRARY CARDS

#1 Miguel Fernandez
Incident at Hawk's Hill by Allan W. Eckert/
No, David! by David Shannon

#2 Akimi Hughes
One Fish Two Fish Red Fish Blue Fish
by Dr Seuss/Nine Stories by J. D. Salinger

#3 Andrew Peckleman
Six Days of the Condor by James Grady/
Eight Cousins by Louisa May Alcott

#4 Bridgette Wadge
Tales of a Fourth Grade Nothing
by Judy Blume/

Harry Potter and the
Philosopher's Stone by J. K. Rowling

#5 Sierra Russell
The Egypt Game by Zilpha Keatley Snyder/
The Westing Game by Ellen Raskin

#6 Yasmeen Smith-Snyder
Around the World in Eighty Days
by Jules Verne/The Yak Who Yelled Yuck
by Carol Pugliano-Martin

#7 Sean Keegan
Olivia by Ian Falconer/Unreal! by Paul Jennings

#8 Haley Daley
Turtle in Paradise by Jennifer L. Holm/
A Wrinkle in Time by Madeleine L'Engle

#9 Rose Vermette
All-of-a-Kind Family by Sydney Taylor/
Scat by Carl Hiaasen

#10 Kayla Corson
Anna to the Infinite Power
by Mildred Ames/Where the Sidewalk
Ends by Shel Silverstein

#12 Kyle Keeley
I Love You, Stinky Face by Lisa McCourt/
The Napping House by Audrey Wood

"Wow," said Haley. "What a mess."

"Tell me about it," said Akimi.

"I don't think it's another author-title game," said Sierra, "like up on the Wonder Dome."

"Huh?" said Haley.

"Long story," said Miguel. "We'll save it for later."

"What we need," said Kyle, "is some kind of clue to show us how to unscramble this list. Remember what Dr Zinchenko said when the game started: 'Your library cards are the keys to everything you will need.' This clue is the big one, guys. We need to crack it."

That's when Mr Lemoncello popped his head in the door.

"Hello, hope I'm not interrupting. We have twenty minutes till the doors open upstairs. Anybody up for an Extreme Challenge?"

48

"In case you forgot," said Mr Lemoncello, "Extreme Challenges are extremely challenging and sometimes extremely dangerous."

"Is Charles doing one?" asked Akimi.

"He might. I'm going to ask him if he'd like to next."

Mr Lemoncello had changed out of his judge's costume into some kind of cat burglar outfit – black pants, ribbed black turtleneck and sporty black beret.

"Is that costume a clue?" asked Haley. "Because it goes with the whole bandit theme."

"Don't know. But Dr Zinchenko told me to wear it for the big finale. Is there going to be a finale?"

"Maybe with Charles," mumbled Kyle. "We're sort of stuck."

"At least till eleven," added Sierra. "That's when the most important clue will appear on the ceiling."

"Really?" said Mr Lemoncello. "That Dr Zinchenko. The woman knows how to build suspense."

"So let's do the Extreme Challenge," said Haley. "What do we have to lose?"

"Um, the whole game," said Akimi.

"Not for all of us," said Kyle. "I'll do the challenge. After all, I'm the team captain."

"You are?" said Haley.

"We had an election," said Akimi. "Yesterday."

"Oh. Cool."

"But, Kyle," said Miguel, "if you blow the Extreme Challenge, you lose, bro."

"Not if my team wins."

"No," said Mr Lemoncello. "If you lose, Kyle, you *lose*. You will not be allowed to share in the big prize."

"Fine."

"I'm going with you," said Haley.

"No, you're not," said Mr Lemoncello.

"I have to. Look, we both know I'd be a *fabulous* spokesmodel for your games and stuff, but I can't just glom on to everything Kyle and his team have already dug up. I have to earn my place on this team."

"Sorry, Haley. Extreme Challenges are, and always will be, solo efforts."

"But . . ."

Mr Lemoncello held up his hand. "No buts. Kyle must face this challenge alone. However . . ."

"Yes?"

"The rest of you can watch his progress on the video screens and cheer him on over the intercom system. You are a cheerleader, aren't you, Haley?"

"Yep," said Kyle. "But she's never cheered for me."

"Well, I will this time. I promise."

"Excellent," said Mr Lemoncello. "By the way, Kyle, there is no backing out once you commit to the challenge."

"Fine," said Kyle. "Let's do it."

"Go, Kyle, gooooo!" shouted Haley.

Akimi flinched. "Um, a warning next time . . . please?"

"Sorry."

Mr Lemoncello touched his ear again. "Here is your Extreme Challenge. Dr Zinchenko tells me:

" '*The answer you seek . . .*' "

He paused to listen.

" ' *. . . the key to this code . . .*
is a memory box . . .
that holds the mother lode.' "

"What?"

Mr Lemoncello shrugged. "Sorry. I don't write 'em. I only recite 'em. Wait. There's more:

" '*Forget the Industrial Revolution;*
my first idea is your certain solution.' "

246

The room was silent.

Mr Lemoncello touched his ear once more and continued, " 'And now, it's time for the addendum.' "

"Huh?"

"A last-minute addition:

" *'The box had been here*
but now it is there.
Poor Kyle. Your fate
is up in the air.' "

Mr Lemoncello stood there grinning. For several seconds.

"Is that it?" said Kyle.

"Yes. Find what you're looking for before the first-floor doors open, and it is yours. Fail, and you, Kyle, will be eliminated from the game, and your team, due to that series of unfortunate events, will be forced to struggle on without you. Good luck. You have fifteen minutes."

And Mr Lemoncello left the room.

"Dude," said Miguel, shaking his head. "You are so dead."

"Wait a second," said Haley. "I think I know how to find what Mr Lemoncello was talking about!"

"You do?" said Kyle.

"I better. I'm the one who moved it from 'here' to 'there'!"

49

"Now then, Charles," said Mr Lemoncello, "would you like to utilize any of your remaining lifelines? Perhaps an Extreme Challenge? An Ask an Expert?"

"Yes, sir," said Charles. "And may I just say, it's kind of you to come in here and ask me that question."

"Well, it's cloudy with a chance of meatballs and I had nothing better to do."

"Pardon?"

"Nothing. Just a brief flight of fancy, my mind sailing off past the phantom tollbooth. So, which lifeline would you like to use?"

"My Ask an Expert, sir."

"Fine. See Mrs Tobin at the main desk. I must go to my office to monitor Kyle's Extreme Challenge."

"What's he doing?"

"Trying to beat you. Tootles!"

Mr Lemoncello raised his beret by its stem, turned on his heel, and headed for one of the bookcases on the far side of the rotunda.

Charles watched him tilt back the head on a bust and press a red button in the middle of what would have been the man's neck. A door-sized section of the bookcase swung open. Mr Lemoncello stepped into the darkness. The bookcase swung shut.

Charles hurried to the librarian's desk at the centre of the Rotunda Reading Room.

"Mrs Tobin?" He clapped his hands. "Mrs Tobin? Chop-chop. I'm in a bit of a rush. The doors upstairs will be open in thirteen minutes. Mrs Tobin?"

The holographic librarian finally appeared.

"Good morning, CHARLES. How may I help you?"

"I need to use my Ask an Expert."

"Very well. Whom do you wish to consult with?"

"Someone who knows his way around a library."

"If that is all you require, CHARLES, perhaps I can be of assistance."

"I need to talk to my uncle Jimmy."

"Your uncle Jimmy? Could you please be more specific?"

"Yes. Of course. James F. Willoughby the third."

"*The* James F. Willoughby the third?"

"Yes, ma'am."

"The *head librarian* of the *Library of Congress* in *Washington, D.C.,* is your uncle?"

"That's right. If my mother's brother, Uncle Jimmy, the top librarian in all of America, can't help me find the one book I'm looking for, nobody can!"

50

"The memory box is down in the Stacks," Haley told Kyle.

So he raced down to the basement. The very long, very wide cellar was just as he remembered it: filled with tidy rows of floor-to-ceiling shelving units.

Kyle looked up at the closest security camera.

"Where to next?"

"I hid it way over on the far side," said Haley through the ceiling speakers. "On a shelf near that horrible book-sorting machine."

Kyle hurried up the centre aisle.

Suddenly, a heavy metal bookcase thundered in from the right, sliding like it was on roller skates.

"Watch it!" shouted Haley.

The bookcase skidded to a screeching halt, blocking Kyle's path forward.

"Go left," suggested Miguel.

The whole team was watching and cheering him on.

Kyle went left.

And another steel shelving unit shuffled in from the side.

"Jump back!" shouted Akimi.

The shelf slammed to a stop two inches in front of Kyle's feet.

"Kyle? You OK?"

"Yeah."

"This is like the hedge maze in the Triwizard Tournament," said Sierra.

"Huh?"

"Harry Potter. Book four. *Goblet of Fire*."

"Right. Need to read that one, too."

Kyle, of course, realized he'd just discovered the most "extreme" part of his Extreme Challenge. Each one of the sliding floor-to-ceiling bookcases was loaded down with heavy cardboard cartons, books, or metal storage bins. They probably weighed several tons each. If Kyle was in the wrong place when a shelving unit came shooting in from the side, he'd be flattened like a pancake under a steamroller.

"Warning," announced the official-sounding lady in the ceiling. "You have twelve minutes to complete this challenge."

He had to keep going. Like Mr Lemoncello said, there was no turning back now. Unless, of course, he wanted to go home a loser.

Ha! Never!

Kyle jogged up an alleyway between two walls of bookshelves.

"Left turn!" Haley shouted. "Now!"

The wall on Kyle's right swung open, revealing six swivelling sections, each pivoting panel maybe twenty feet long, all skittering sideways and gliding backwards to create new walls and reconfigured pathways.

"You've only got like ten more yards to go," coached Haley.

Kyle weaved his way around the randomly shuffling shelves.

But as soon as he was on any kind of straightaway, the walls started to rearrange themselves again.

Finally, Kyle scooted down a corridor so tight he had to turn sideways to squeeze through. The walls stuttered to a stop.

And the voice made another announcement. "Warning. You have eight minutes to complete this challenge."

"I'm trapped!" Kyle shouted. "There's no exit."

None of his teammates said anything for a real long time.

Finally, Sierra's voice rang out from the overhead speakers.

"Put your hand on the right wall," she said.

"What? Why?"

"When I was little, I played a lot of maze games. If the walls are connected, all you have to do is keep one hand in contact with one wall at all times and eventually you'll reach the exit or return to the entrance."

"Do it," coached Akimi.

"It'll work, bro," added Miguel.

So Kyle kept his right hand firmly planted on the right wall of shelves and started inching his way forward.

"Go, Kyle!" cheered Haley. "Hug that wall! Hug that wall!"

The passageway widened. Kyle kept his hand glued to the right wall and went around corners, through switchbacks, until finally, he stepped into an opening near the book return conveyor belt.

"You made it!" shouted Haley. "Whoo-hoo!"

All the shelves streamed back into their orderly church pew positions.

"Good," said Kyle. "Getting out should be easier than getting in. Where's the box, Haley?"

"I put it on the shelf."

"Which one?"

"That one."

"Warning," announced the calm female voice in the ceiling again. "You have THREE MINUTES to complete this challenge."

Kyle stared up at a nearby camera. "Um, Haley? What exactly am I looking for?"

"A cardboard box. In a drawer."

"OK. There are like a billion of those . . ."

"I flagged it with a piece of pink tissue."

Kyle raced to a shelf.

"TWO MINUTES," announced the calm lady.

"This one?" said Kyle.

"Yes! Look in the steel drawer."

"I thought you said it was cardboard . . ."

"It is. Open the lid. Not that lid. The other one."

"This one?"

"No! The one under it!"

"ONE MINUTE."

"Hurry, Kyle!"

"I'm hurrying."

"Flip it open."

Kyle did as he was told. He flipped up the lid on a steel drawer and found a battered boot box.

Every member of Kyle's team shouted the same thing: "Grab it!"

"And run!" added Akimi.

Kyle did.

He tucked the boot box under his arm and ran like he had never run before.

He sprinted across the basement floor. He raced up the steps, two at a time.

When he hit the rotunda, his heart was pounding against his ribs.

"THIRTY SECONDS."

He speed-skated across the marble floor. It was so slippery he lost his balance.

He fell forward.

Dropped the box.

It flew out of his hands, hit the slick floor, and slid like a hockey puck across the threshold into Community Meeting Room B.

A buzzer sounded.

"Time is up," announced the calm voice.

"Yo," shouted Miguel, "you made it, bro!"

And Kyle started breathing again.

51

Having made his request, all Charles could do was wait.

"Apparently," said Mr Lemoncello when he came back into the rotunda, "your uncle Jimmy is a very, *very* busy man. Reminds me of a spider I once knew. But it is a Sunday morning. We will attempt to track him down at home."

"Thank you, sir. I told Uncle Jimmy to stand by. That I might need him this weekend."

"And now – *WHOOSH!* He's as elusive as the wind in the willows. You'll have to discuss this with him the next time your family gets together for Thanksgiving dinner. Now, if you will excuse me, it is currently nine-fifty-eight a.m. Almost time to reopen the Dewey decimal chambers."

Mr Lemoncello opened a filing cabinet and pulled out a megaphone.

"Is there some room you should be ready to run to? Isn't there some clue or book you need to go find?"

"Just one," said Charles. "And I need my uncle Jimmy to tell me which one it is. Will you keep looking for him? Please."

"Of course." Mr Lemoncello pointed to a smudge on Charles's shirt. "If you like, I will also have Al Capone do your shirts."

All Charles could do was nod, smile and wonder when Al Capone had opened a laundry.

52

"Everyone, please pay very close attention," cried Mr Lemoncello through a squealing, screeching megaphone. "The Dewey decimal doors are now open and, unlike Tuck, this game will not be everlasting. Therefore, it is time to race upstairs like the rats of NIMH!"

Kyle and his teammates heard Mr Lemoncello's announcement but stayed inside Community Meeting Room B so they could examine the dusty old boot box.

"It's from when Mr Lemoncello was our age," said Haley. "Here. I'm pretty sure this is what we need." She handed Kyle a large manila envelope sealed up with tons of tape. "First and Worst Idea Ever" had been scribbled on the front.

"Awesome," said Kyle as he started undoing the tape. "The clue said his first idea might be our best solution."

Inside the envelope were a stack of cards, a bunch of rubber stamps, an ink pad and a sheet of three-ring-binder paper filled with a fifth grader's sloppy handwriting.

Kyle read out loud what the young Luigi Lemoncello had written: "'Presenting First Letters: the Amazingly Incredible Secret Code Game'."

Haley held up some of the cards. Each one showed a cartoony drawing and a single letter: Apple = A, Bee = B, Carrot = C and so on.

Kyle continued reading: "'Want to send your friend a secret message to meet you after school? Just use your super-secret rubber stamps.'"

Miguel examined a couple of the wood-handled stamps. "The stamps match the cards."

"So how exactly do you use this junk to tell your friends to meet you after school?" asked Akimi.

"This is so bad," said Kyle. "'Moon, Elephant, Elephant, Tiger. Moon, Elephant. Apple, Flamingo . . .'"

Akimi held up her hand. "OK. Stop. I get it."

"Maybe it was for little kids," said Sierra.

"Definitely," said Kyle. "Because anybody over the age of six could crack this code in like ten seconds."

And then he froze.

"This is it!"

He went to the wall with the list of library cards. "What would happen if we played First Letters with these book titles?"

260

BOOKS/AUTHORS ON THE BACKS OF
LIBRARY CARDS

#1 Miguel Fernandez
Incident at Hawk's Hill by Allan W. Eckert/
No, David! by David Shannon

#2 Akimi Hughes
One Fish Two Fish Red Fish Blue Fish
by Dr Seuss/Nine Stories by J. D. Salinger

#3 Andrew Peckleman
Six Days of the Condor by James Grady/
Eight Cousins by Louisa May Alcott

#4 Bridgette Wadge
Tales of a Fourth Grade Nothing
by Judy Blume/Harry Potter and the
Philosopher's Stone by J. K. Rowling

#5 Sierra Russell
The Egypt Game by Zilpha Keatley Snyder/
The Westing Game by Ellen Raskin

#6 Yasmeen Smith-Snyder
Around the World in Eighty Days
by Jules Verne/The Yak Who Yelled Yuck
by Carol Pugliano-Martin

#7 Sean Keegan
Olivia by Ian Falconer/Unreal! by Paul Jennings

#8 Haley Daley
Turtle in Paradise by Jennifer L. Holm/
A Wrinkle in Time by Madeleine L'Engle

#9 Rose Vermette
All-of-a-Kind Family by Sydney Taylor/
Scat by Carl Hiaasen

#10 Kayla Corson
Anna to the Infinite Power
by Mildred Ames/Where the Sidewalk
Ends by Shel Silverstein

#11 UNKNOWN/CHARLES CHILTINGTON

#12 Kyle Keeley
I Love You, Stinky Face by Lisa McCourt/
The Napping House by Audrey Wood

"OK," said Miguel, moving to a clean space on the wall. "Here are the first letters of all the titles."

I N O N S E T H T T A T O U T A A S A W ? ? I T

"It still makes no sense," said Akimi.

"Wait a second," said Sierra. "If the title starts with an article, drop that word, and use the letter from the second word."

"Got it," said Miguel.

INONSETHEWAYOUTWASAW??IN

"OK," said Akimi. "It's making some sense."
She went to the board and broke Miguel's string of letters into words.

I/NON/SET/HE/WAY/OUT/WAS/A/W??/IN

"Hang on," said Kyle. "It could be . . ."

IN/ON/SE/THE/WAY/OUT/WAS/A/W??/IN

"What's 'In on se'?" said Akimi.
"Wait! Look!" said Miguel. "The books on the second and third library cards actually start with *numbers*!"
Kyle grabbed a marker:

IN/1968/THE/WAY/OUT/WAS/A/W??/IN

"Hang on," said Haley. "You know all those questions in the trivia contest Friday? I did so badly, I Googled a bunch of them later that night. They were all from 1968."
"You guys?" said Sierra. "I did some research, too.

Mr Lemoncello was born in 1956. That means he turned twelve in 1968."

"OK . . ." said Akimi. "Is this something besides a fun fact to know and tell?"

"You bet it is," said Kyle. "Nineteen sixty-eight is key. And we don't need Charles's library card to finish this phrase." He went to the whiteboard.

IN 1968, THE WAY OUT WAS A WAY IN.

"So what happened in 1968?" said Haley.

"Was that when *Charlie and the Chocolate Factory* came out?" asked Miguel.

"No," said Sierra. "Nineteen sixty-four."

"So what's up with the candy clue from the Art and Artifacts Room?"

"We messed up," said Akimi. "We need to go back and find a new rhyme for 'Andy'!"

"Really?" said Haley. "I thought he got kicked out for cheating."

"Another long story," said Miguel.

"For later," said Kyle. "Right now, we need to be on the second floor!"

53

Back in the Art & Artifacts Room, Kyle felt confident they were pretty close to figuring out, well, whatever it was they were supposed to figure out.

How it would help them escape from the library was still anybody's guess.

"It's ten-forty-four," said Akimi. "The last clue should pop up on the Wonder Dome in sixteen minutes."

"OK, you guys," said Kyle. "Spread out. We need a new rhyme for 'Andy'."

"This model of the bank building came in *handy*," added Miguel.

"The Dandy Bandits!" shouted Akimi, once again studying the display of hats.

"Yes!" said Haley, pulling off her shoe so she could show everybody her clue card.

 **+ ITS**

"Bandits! I found this in the three hundreds room."

"That's the room clue we're waiting for," said Kyle.

"Because the Dewey decimal number for True Crime books always starts with the number three," said Miguel. "When we find that book, it'll tell us how and where the 'bandits crawled in in 1968.'"

"Listen to this, you guys," said Akimi. She read a placard in the display case: "'This plaid fedora from *1968* was worn by bank robber Leopold Loblolly, one of the notorious *Dandy* Bandits.'"

"Loblolly!" Miguel shouted.

"The smell-a-vision clue," said Kyle. "That's why everything kept smelling like pine trees."

"Loblolly was one of the pine trees in the answer Mr Lemoncello gave you guys!" said Haley.

"Whoop-whoop-whoop," said Mr Lemoncello as, banana shoes squeaking, he stepped into the room. "Well done, Miss Daley . . . and Miss Hughes."

"See?" said Akimi. "I was right the first time we came in here. I said 'dandy' and everybody else said, 'Noooo, *candy*. Willy Wonka . . .'"

"Yes, it's all coming back to me," said Mr Lemoncello.

"Nineteen sixty-eight. I was pondering an idea for a game at the old public library."

"And," said Kyle, "you were so totally focused, you didn't hear the police sirens screaming past the library as they raced to the Gold Leaf Bank . . ."

"The blackbird was from Alexandriaville," said Sierra. "The police siren wail was from that day."

Miguel finished that thought: "When the Dandy Bandits tried to crawl into the bank!"

"My goodness," said Mr Lemoncello. "How could you kids know all that?"

"From the game clues," said Kyle, "and from the story Dr Zinchenko told us on Friday night when somebody asked her why a library building needed a bank vault door."

"She was already feeding us clues!" said Akimi.

"The time is now ELEVEN a.m.," announced the ceiling lady. "This game will end in ONE hour."

"Come on," said Kyle, heading for the door. "It's the eleventh hour. We need to go check out the Wonder Dome again."

They raced to the balcony.

"There it is!" said Sierra.

"364 point 1092!" shouted Miguel.

"Whoo-hoo!" cried Akimi. "We're gonna win!"

54

On the ground floor, Charles was at long last video chatting with his uncle, James Willoughby III, the librarian of Congress, who had finally shown up for the Ask an Expert call.

"Sorry for the delay, Charles."

"That's OK, Uncle Jimmy," Charles said, straining to smile and not scream.

"The time is now ELEVEN a.m.," announced the annoyingly placid lady in the ceiling. "This game will end in ONE hour."

Charles had to hustle.

"Sir, I know you're a very important, very busy man, so I just have one quick question: if I were a book on true crimes in the state of Ohio, where would you shelve me?"

"Library of Congress classification?"

"No, sir. Dewey decimal."

"Ah. Easy. 364 point 1. What comes after the one will depend, of course, on how many books a library . . ."

Charles didn't stick around to hear the rest of his uncle's answer.

He took off running for the closest spiral staircase up to the first floor. As he ascended the steps, two at a time, he saw Kyle Keeley and his entire entourage running down a staircase from the second floor.

Charles reached the first-floor balcony before them.

He darted around the bend, past the door to the 500s room, the 400s.

Keeley and his crew were coming from the opposite direction, but Charles reached the door to the 300s room before them.

He swiped his library card, yanked on the handle, and dashed into the room.

He scanned the shelves and headed to his right.

He heard Keeley enter the room.

Glancing over his shoulder, Charles saw Keeley go left.

Charles dashed up an aisle between bookcases. He read the number at the end of each row of shelves.

310.

320.

330.

One of those robots with the book baskets came rumbling across his path, but Charles was able to dodge it.

340.

350.

Keeley's footsteps pounded up the passageway on the other side of the shelving units to his left.

In the middle of the 300s room, they entered an open space with a judge's bench and witness box.

Charles was getting closer to the True Crime section.

But so was Kyle.

Charles saw Keeley read something off his palm.

He had the whole call number!

It was time to change tactics.

Charles hung back and let Keeley take the lead.

Kyle rushed towards a bookcase.

Charles sprinted after him.

"Got it!" Kyle shouted as he reached for a book on the shelf.

But before he could completely pull it out, Charles grabbed hold of the book, too.

They both yanked it off the shelf.

Kyle had the spine; Charles had hold of the top.

They tugged it back and forth.

While they wrestled with the book, Keeley's teammates caught up to them.

"Careful, Kyle," cried Sierra Russell. "Don't hurt the book."

Charles grinned. Keeley, the sentimental sap, was listening to the silly, bookish girl and easing up on his grip.

Giving Charles his chance.

He body-checked Keeley. Slammed into him with his

shoulder. Sent him flying, the book tumbling. Charles snatched it off the floor.

He had the book. He quickly flipped through the table of contents. Saw chapter 11 was about a robbery at the Gold Leaf Bank in Alexandriaville.

He knew he'd won the game.

Charles used his free hand to slap an "L" on his forehead.

"Loser," he sneered at Keeley.

A tiger roared, a whistle blew, and Mr Lemoncello entered the room, accompanied by Clarence, Clement and what looked like a rare Bengal tiger.

"Mr Chiltington?"

Charles smiled. He knew Mr Lemoncello was about to congratulate him for defying the odds and winning the game. He had single-handedly defeated Kyle Keeley's entire team! "Yes, sir, Mr Lemoncello?"

"Do you remember Dr Zinchenko's number one rule?"

"You bet, sir. No food or drink except in the Book Nook Cafe."

"No," said Mr Lemoncello, touching the tip of his nose and making a buzzer noise. "Dr Z? Tell him what he should've said."

Dr Zinchenko's voice purred out of the ceiling speakers. "Be gentle. With each other and, most especially, the library's books and exhibits."

"I know," said Charles. "That's why I had to stop Kyle

Keeley. He was ready to rip the cover off this poor book. Heck, sir, everybody at school knows that Kyle Keeley is a maniac. He'll do anything to win a game."

Mr Lemoncello turned to Keeley.

"Is that true, Kyle? Would you actually destroy property if it stood between you and your prize?"

"W-well, sir . . ."

Keeley was stammering. The fool didn't know how to lie.

Charles quickly opened the book to chapter 11 and slipped in his library card to bookmark the location.

"You should ask Keeley about the window he broke, sir."

Mr Lemoncello turned to face Charles again.

"The window?"

"Yes, sir. The whole school heard about it. See, Kyle Keeley and his two brothers were playing some sort of wild scavenger hunt game and . . ."

Mr Lemoncello pointed at the book. "That's clever. You use your library card as a bookmark?"

"Yes, sir, I sure do," said Charles, turning on the charm. "Of course, I can't take full credit for such a clever idea. On Friday night, I saw Sierra Russell doing it and . . ."

"You told Andrew Peckleman to 'borrow' her card."

Charles blinked. Several times. "I beg your pardon?"

"You broke Dr Zinchenko's number one rule. You

were not gentle with your teammate Andrew. In fact, you bullied him into stealing Miss Russell's library card, which you knew she always used as a bookmark."

"No, sir. I did not."

"Yes, Charles. You did." Mr Lemoncello touched his right ear. "In fact, Dr Zinchenko has spent the past few hours combing through security tapes, and guess what she just found?"

Charles heard his own voice ringing out of the ceiling speakers:

"Have you noticed what Sierra Russell uses for a bookmark?"

"No."

"That was Andrew," said Mr Lemoncello. "This is you again."

"Her library card, which, of course, doubles as a key card for Meeting Room B. Find a way to borrow it."

"You told Andrew to steal Sierra's library card."

"How could you record that?" said Charles. "I was whispering!"

"And *I* have very good microphones. You're done, Charles. Dr Zinchenko? Tell our departing guest what he has just won."

"Absolutely nothing," said the voice of the Russian librarian. "But please, Mr L, tell Charles the correct answer to the final pictogram."

"Ah, yes!" Mr Lemoncello reached into his back

pocket, pulled out a four-by-four card, and showed it to Charles.

Charles stood there fuming.

"Anyone care to help Charles out?"

"Hmmm," said Kyle. "Is it 'six eat'?"

"You are very close," said Mr Lemoncello.

There was a pause and then Haley laughed. "Did it come after the football player?"

"Yeah," said Charles. "So?"

"Andrew was right all along," said Haley. "The football player clue wasn't 'past', it was 'nineteen'."

Mr Lemoncello shifted into his game show voice. "So, Haley Daley, would you care to solve the puzzle?"

"Sure: 'You can walk out the way bandits crawled in in nineteen six ate.'"

"I don't get it," said Charles.

"Nineteen, six-ate," said Akimi. "You know: 1968."

"Ah, yes," said Mr Lemoncello. "The year *From the Mixed-Up Files of Mrs Basil E. Frankweiler* won the Newbery Medal for excellence in children's literature. Another clue you completely missed, Charles."

"Wow," said Miguel. "And I thought Chiltingtons never lose."

"There's a first time for everything," said Mr Lemoncello. "Clarence? Clement? Kindly escort young Mr Chiltington from the building."

"Buh-bye," said Akimi. "There goes this game's biggest loser."

55

"Open it!" Akimi said to Kyle. "We only have like forty minutes to figure out how Loblolly and the Dandy Bandits crawled into the bank back in 1968!"

Kyle flipped through *True Crime Ohio* to the place where Charles had slipped in his bookmark.

"Well?" said Miguel.

" 'Chapter Eleven. The Dandy Bandits Burrow into a Bank Vault.' "

"Even though thou should not steal," said Akimi.

"And I'll bet they crawled in, right?" said Haley.

" 'The clever thieves,' " Kyle read from the book, " 'took up residence in an abandoned dress factory next door to the Gold Leaf Bank and spent weeks tunnelling from its basement into the bank vault.' "

"Which," said Miguel, "according to those old

blueprints I found, was down where the book-sorting machine is now."

"That explains the first clue," said Kyle. "The book title was *Get to Know Your Local Library*. Dr Zinchenko meant we needed to get to know *this* library. This also explains why she wanted us to read those Sherlock Holmes stories."

"'The Adventure of the Red-Headed League,'" said Sierra. "The story about robbers tunnelling into a bank from the building next door."

Kyle nodded. "Dr Zinchenko told me *she* had just reread it. I'll bet that's where she got the idea for this whole game."

"Hey, Charles should've stuck with crawling through sewers like he did in that video game," joked Miguel. "He might've found the Dandy Bandits' tunnel before we did."

"Come on, you guys," said Haley. "We need to be back in the basement."

"I'm coming with you," said Mr Lemoncello. "I just have to see how this story ends!"

Clutching the *True Crime* book against his chest, Kyle led the way down to the Stacks.

"Why are you bringing that book?" asked Akimi.

"We'll put it on that conveyor belt thing," Kyle explained. "Whatever basket the scanner sends it to, I'm guessing that's where we'll find our 'black square'."

"Our shortcut out of the library!"

277

"Exactly."

As the team trooped down the steps to the basement, Mr Lemoncello turned to Kyle and said, "So, Mr Keeley, did you have fun this weekend?"

"Yeah."

"Good. Congratulations, Miss Hughes, it seems *you* have already won."

Akimi sort of blushed.

"What do you mean?" asked Kyle.

"In her essay, your extremely good friend wrote, and I quote: 'I want to see the new library so I can tell my friend Kyle Keeley how cool it is.'"

"You wrote your essay about me?"

"Maybe," mumbled Akimi.

"Wow," said Kyle. "No one's ever done that before."

"Well, no one's ever going to do it again if you blow our chance at winning this thing. So can we please stop yakking and find our way out of here?"

"Works for me."

"Warning," said the calm voice in the ceiling speakers. "This game will terminate in THIRTY minutes."

Everybody moved a little faster.

Fortunately, when the group reached the basement, the floor-to-ceiling bookshelves didn't start sliding into another maze formation.

"The automatic book sorter is straight up this path, near the far wall," said Kyle.

They made it to the conveyor belt.

"From what I remember from the old blueprints," said Miguel, "the vault was right here, in the same spot as this machine."

"OK, you guys," said Kyle. "Whatever robo-basket this book ends up in is probably sitting right on top of the entrance to the tunnel."

"Here goes everything." Kyle placed *True Crime Ohio* into the array of crisscrossing beams.

Nothing happened.

"What's going on?" cried Miguel. "Why isn't it working?"

"Maybe this book isn't heavy enough." Kyle pushed down on the cover of the book a bit.

Still nothing.

They stared, dumbfounded, at the book sitting on the immobile belt.

"It wouldn't *stop* moving yesterday," muttered Haley.

"That's it!" cried Akimi. She hurried to the wall and flipped the emergency shutoff switch back to the "on" position.

Several red laser scanners sprang to life under the book drop slot.

The belt started moving. Slowly.

The single book worked its way down the line like a

candy bar on a wrapping machine. When it reached the third robo-basket from the end, a set of rollers popped up and shunted the book off to the side into the waiting wire basket.

The conveyor belt stopped rolling. The robo-cart rolled away.

Nothing else happened.

"That's it?"

"Warning," said the calm voice. "This game will terminate in TWENTY minutes."

"It didn't work," said Haley.

"We're toast," added Akimi.

"Wait," said Kyle, pointing to a square tile on the floor where the robo-basket had been. It was glowing, like one of the touch-screen computers in the desks upstairs. "It says 'Howdy. Dü you like fun games? Get Reddy.'"

"Excellent!" Akimi giggled. Then she and Kyle cracked up, remembering the box tops from their first puzzle in the Board Room on Saturday morning.

"Now it says we're going to get an anagram," said Kyle.

"My favourite kind of cookies," said Mr Lemoncello.

"OK, everybody," said Kyle. "Gather round. Get ready."

Kyle, Akimi, Sierra, Miguel and Haley knelt on the floor in a circle around the square. Mr Lemoncello hovered behind them.

"Here we go," said Kyle as game instructions scrolled across the screen.

A sixty-second clock popped up at the bottom of the screen. And then a four-by-four Boggle jumble of letters:

"Luigi L. Lemoncello," mumbled Kyle.

The sixty-second clock started ticking down.

Sierra shouted out, "Lemon!" and a *ding* sounded from the speaker above. The five teammates started shouting out words:

"Cello!"

"Eon!"

"Elm!"

"Lion!"

"Mole!"

"Leg!"

"Oil!"

281

"Thirty seconds left," said Mr Lemoncello.

"One!"

"Cell!"

"Cone!"

"Lone!"

"Glen!"

"Lime!"

"Eh, mole."

"We already said that."

"Melon."

"That's fifteen," said the voice in the ceiling.

"Um . . ."

"Ten seconds left."

"Anybody?"

"Five."

"Four."

"Colonel!" shouted Haley.

The computer screen flashed "Congratulations!" and "Winners!"

Somewhere, a game show audience cheered, fireworks rockets whistled through the air, and several geese honked out a "Hooray!"

"Please stand back," said the soothing voice in the ceiling.

Kyle and his teammates did as they were told.

"Warning," the voice continued. "This game will terminate in FIFTEEN minutes."

"We still need to get out, you guys!" said Akimi. "Hurry, floor. Do something!"

The eight tiles surrounding the glowing tablet also started to glow. First yellow, then orange, then purple.

"Our secret square," said Akimi.

There was a series of clicks, and the tiles began folding up on themselves and retracting into the floor, opening up like an origami trapdoor.

"Look," said Haley, "there's steps."

Mr Lemoncello peered down into the hole at the well-lit staircase and tunnel. "My, my. Dr Zinchenko has certainly cleaned things up since Mr Loblolly was here."

"Of course she did," said Haley. "So we 'can walk out the way bandits crawled in in nineteen six-ate'."

"Hurry, everybody!" said Mr Lemoncello. "I don't want to be late to my own birthday party."

56

Kyle led the way up the tunnel and brought his team (plus
Mr Lemoncello) into an empty basement filled with mannequins and cardboard boxes.

"This must be the cellar of one of the clothing shops in
Old Town," said Kyle.

"The Fitting Factory," said Haley, reading a tag on a
shipping crate. "It's one of my faves."

"And," said Sierra, "back in 1968, it was the real dress
factory that Leopold Loblolly and the Dandy Bandits
used."

"There's some steps over here," said Miguel, climbing
a wooden staircase. "And a door." He jiggled the knob.
"Oh, man – it's locked."

Kyle looked up at the dingy casement windows, about
ten feet above the cellar floor.

He couldn't help grinning.

It reminded him of another game he'd won once. This time, he'd just have to reverse things a little.

"Help me drag over a couple cartons," Kyle said to Miguel. "We can stack them on top of each other underneath this window."

After they built a step unit out of boxes, Kyle climbed up and examined the window latch.

"Great," he said.

"Don't tell me," said Akimi. "Another game?"

"Yep. There's a combination lock – the kind with four wheels of random letters."

"Warning," said the voice.

"What?" said Akimi. "Dr Zinchenko put loudspeakers in this basement, too?"

"This game will terminate in FOUR minutes."

"Yo, open the lock, Kyle!" said Miguel.

"Hang on. It's some kind of word game."

"Is there a clue?" asked Haley.

"Of course." Kyle read the tiny slip of paper taped to the glass. " 'Once you learn how to do this, you will be forever free.' "

Everyone started laughing.

This last puzzle was ridiculously easy.

"Ready, children?" said Mr Lemoncello. "All together now!"

And they all shouted it at the same time: "READ!"

285

Kyle thumbed the wheels to spell R-E-A-D. The lock clicked. The window opened.

And this time, he didn't need to shatter any glass to win the game.

Kyle and Mr Lemoncello stood on top of the highest box and helped the others up and out of the basement.

When Haley crawled through the window frame, someone in the crowd that had gathered around the library for the game's big finale saw her and started screaming.

"Look! It's Haley Daley! She's the first one out. She won! With just two minutes to go!"

"Nuh-uh!" Kyle heard Haley shout in her perky cheerleader voice. "I'm just one member of a super-amazing team. We're all winners. Whoo-hoo!"

When Akimi climbed through the window, the crowd chanted her name.

"How do you people know my name?" Kyle heard her say. "Dad? Did you tell them?"

Sierra Russell was set to crawl out next.

"Mr Lemoncello?"

"Yes, Sierra?"

"What time does the library open tomorrow?"

"For you, Sierra, nine a.m.!"

Smiling, she stepped into their hands and climbed out the window.

Kyle felt bad when Sierra stood up on the sidewalk. Who was out there to cheer for her?

But then he heard Haley shout, "Hey, you guys. You gotta meet our amazing new friend, Sierra Russell! She's so smart, she could tell you who wrote the phone book!"

The crowd went crazy. "Sierra! Sierra! Sierra!"

"OK," said Kyle, "you're next, Miguel."

"And, Miguel," said Mr Lemoncello, "if your summer schedule permits it, I'd love for you to head up my team of Lemoncello Library Aides."

"Thank you, sir. It'd be an honour."

"And please invite Mr Peckleman to join you."

"But Andrew thinks this library is stupid."

"All the more reason for him to spend time getting to know us a little better. Now, off you go!"

They gave Miguel a boost up and out the window.

The chanting outside grew even louder.

"Miguel! Miguel! Miguel!"

"You guys?" Miguel shouted. "This library is like a good book. You just gotta check it out!"

The crowd laughed. Kyle groaned.

"You're next, Mr Keeley," said Mr Lemoncello.

"OK. Can I ask one last question?"

"Certainly. And I hope it won't be the last."

"Are you really going to put all of us in your television commercials?"

"Oh, yes. You'll be quite famous."

"Cool."

"Indeed. Who knew spending time in your local library could be such a rewarding experience?"

Kyle smiled. "You did, Mr Lemoncello."

"And now you do, too."

Kyle put his foot in Mr Lemoncello's hands and grabbed hold of the window frame.

"See you at the birthday party, sir!"

"Oh, yes. And you know what, Kyle?"

"What?"

"There might be balloons!"

AUTHOR'S NOTE

Is the game really over?

Maybe not.

There is one more puzzle in the book that wasn't in the story. (Although a clue about how to find it was!)

If you figure out the solution, let me know. Send an email to author@ChrisGrabenstein.com.

THANK YOU . . .

To R. Schuyler Hooke, my longtime editor at Random House, for his incredible patience, faith and input on this project.

To designer Nicole de las Heras and artist Gilbert Ford, who made the book look so darn good.

To my wife, J. J. Myers, who is a terrific first editor.

To Ms Macrina, librarian, and all the folks at P.S. 10 in Brooklyn, whose library gave me the initial inspiration for this story.

To Darrell Robertson, Gail Tobin, Amy Alessio, Erin Downey, Yanna Zinchenko, Scot Smith, and all the other librarians and media specialists I have met in my travels as an author, at public libraries and in schools. When I see how you inspire the love of reading on a daily basis, I realize you are much more amazing and incredible than Mr Lemoncello.

BONUS STUFF

RANDOM CHATTER with
CHRIS GRABENSTEIN

What were you like as a kid?

Kind of chubby. Not very good at sports. But I liked to make my friends (and teachers) laugh. Sometimes I'd do this with comic books that I wrote and drew and passed around in class. I guess those were my first "published" books!

I also spent a lot of time making up imaginary stories. I could play basketball in our driveway all by myself and turn it into the most exciting championship game ever played – complete with sound effects – and do it all in my head. By the way, in those imaginary games, I was *excellent* at sports!

Did you want to be an author when you grew up?

You know, I vaguely remember reading a book in the backseat of the station wagon during my family's long and hot (it was August) car ride from Buffalo, New York, to the beaches of St Petersburg, Florida (where my grandparents lived), and thinking, *I should write a book. About a boy. In the backseat of a station wagon. Dying of heat exhaustion and lack of cupcakes.*

Other than that, I don't really think I ever thought I could be an author when I grew up. I knew I could probably be a writer. But an *author*? I didn't own any tweed sport coats with patches on the elbows.

When I was a kid, I think I wanted to be a famous movie star. Or Johnny Carson. One of those.

Writing wasn't your first career, was it?

Well, I was always writing, but when I moved to New York City right after college (with nothing but seven suitcases and a typewriter I had received as a high school graduation gift), I spent five years doing improvisational comedy down in a basement theatre in Greenwich Village and on the college tour circuit. A guy named Bruce Willis was in one of my comedy troupes. Robin Williams would drop by and hop onstage with us whenever he was in town doing a movie.

When you do improv, you make up scenes and songs right on the spot, based on audience suggestions. For instance, we'd ask the audience for a "personal problem" and then we'd make up an entire instant opera about "BO" or "acne" or whatever they shouted out.

While I was doing improv (and supporting myself with office work), I also had the great good fortune to write for

Jim Henson and the Muppets. What an inspirational man. I think he named his company Henson Associates just so he could have "ha!" as a corporate logo.

I also co-wrote a made-for-TV movie called *The Christmas Gift,* starring John Denver, which first aired on CBS way back in 1986. It's still on TV every year during the holiday season. Usually on the Hallmark Channel. At 3 a.m. I know this because my mother calls me up and tells me.

Then, in 1984, I landed a job on Madison Avenue, writing copy for the J. Walter Thompson advertising agency. I actually got the job by answering a writing aptitude test headlined "Write If You Want Work" that ran in the *New York Times*. It was full of fun questions like "How would you sell a telephone to a Trappist monk who had taken a strict vow of silence?" (I'd convince him he'd need the phone to connect to Monkmail, a new kind of email for silent monks only.)

The creative director of J. Walter Thompson, New York, wrote the test and questions. His name was James Patterson. Yes, *that* James Patterson. Before he became the world-record holder for the Most Number One *New York Times* Bestsellers Ever, he wrote commercials and ran the entire creative department at one of New York's biggest advertising agencies. I learned a lot about writing while working for Mr Patterson, and I'm thrilled to be working with him again, co-authoring books like *I Funny* and *Treasure Hunters*.

What was your inspiration for *Escape from Mr Lemoncello's Library*?

During an author visit to PS 10, a school in Brooklyn, New York, I marvelled at their incredibly beautiful library. The librarian, Ms Macrina, told me that it had been "donated by a very generous benefactor".

That got my mental wheels spinning. *What if . . . a generous benefactor, an eccentric bazillionaire, gave the town where he grew up the most amazingly awesome library ever built?*

By the way, most of my books start with a big *What if . . . ?*

And since, when I was a kid, I loved playing games like Monopoly, Sorry and Risk, I decided to make my eccentric benefactor a wackier version of one of the Parker Brothers, the name behind many of my favourite games.

I think I named him Lemoncello and made him the son of Italian immigrants in honour of my Greek immigrant grandparents, whose last name was Lemonopoulos.

Recently, my mother told me that when she was a little girl growing up in Canton, Ohio, speaking and reading more English than her mom and dad, who were still speaking Greek, she was determined to read every book in the library. The library was where she could learn even more about her family's new home. That's one of the reasons I chose to celebrate the connection between libraries and immigrants in this book.

People have compared Mr Lemoncello to Willy Wonka. Were you thinking of him when you wrote the book?

I was – but only to avoid making Mr Lemoncello too much like Willy Wonka, particularly Gene Wilder's depiction of him in the old movie, which is one of my favourite films. But any time you have an eccentric bazillionaire in a fantastical setting and surround him with kids, it's hard not to be reminded of Willy Wonka. However, Mr Lemoncello has no Oompa-Loompas to help him restock the shelves.

Kyle is very competitive with his brothers, Mike and Curtis. Do you have any brothers?

Yes! Four of them: Tom, Jeff, Steve and Bill. Three of them are now doctors; the other is a lawyer. When we were kids, Tom, the oldest, wasn't a jock like Mike, but he was definitely the Big Brother, the guy we all looked up to, the one who did all the stuff we wished we could do. Jeff, my other older brother, was (and is) a genius like Curtis. I would get straight As at school, but it wasn't really all that impressive. Jeff, who had been in the same class the year before me, got straight A++s.

How did you pick the books featured in Mr Lemoncello's library?

I wanted to make sure that I included classic kids' books as well as more contemporary titles.

Some books were chosen only for their "clue value". They gave me something I needed for a puzzle piece. I tried to pick them from lists of the best middle-grade books or award winners.

Some book titles I made up and tried to make sure they sounded like actual books. A lot of the authors of the made-up books were winners of charity auctions who donated money to various causes to see their names pop up in one of my books.

I had the most fun coming up with famous book titles to slip into Mr Lemoncello's rapid-fire dialogue. Did you catch them all? (Don't worry, there's a complete list coming up!)

What's the best thing you've ever won?

I guess the Lions Club citizenship essay contest when I was in fifth grade. I didn't get to spend the night in a library or a lion's den, but I did receive a nifty medal that my mom and dad had mounted on a tie clip for me. Not that I wore many ties in fifth grade. I was no Charles Chiltington!

I also won a Clifford the Big Red Dog doll for my wife at a boardwalk arcade in New Jersey before a Bruce Springsteen concert. That was cool.

Have you ever been on a scavenger hunt?

Yes, but none as wacky or fun as Mr Lemoncello's Indoor-Outdoor Scavenger Hunt. We used to do them at school, especially near the holidays.

What's your favourite Dewey decimal number?

641.3373. I'm having some right now. Delicious.

Have you ever been to a library as amazing as Mr Lemoncello's?

Actually, a lot of the libraries I visit are even more amazing. I see librarians making great suggestions about books they know kids will love. I see kids working together on school projects, and librarians helping them find the information they need, either online or in the stacks. In one of my favourite libraries, outside Chicago, they have even built Collaboration Stations in their new wing for young adults.

I like Mr Lemoncello's motto: "Knowledge not shared remains unknown." A library is, and always has been, a place where we can come together and share what we know – as the whole human race and as individuals.

If you had as much money as Mr Lemoncello, what would you build with it?

The world's largest and nicest animal rescue shelter with gourmet kibble and tuna for all! Fred, our rescue dog, and Parker, Tiger Lilly and Phoebe Squeak, our rescue cats, had nothing to do with that answer.

BONUS CLUE

Have you solved the extra puzzle mentioned in the author's note? The one that was in the book but wasn't in the story? Here's a hint.

(Of course you have to solve this puzzle to get it!)

BRING THE FUN AND EXCITEMENT OF
MR LEMONCELLO'S LIBRARY
INTO YOUR LIBRARY!

Now you can host a Lemoncello-style scavenger hunt in YOUR library. Working with children's services librarians from the Carroll County Public Library in Finksburg, Maryland, Chris Grabenstein has created Mr Lemoncello's Great Library Escape Game for libraries everywhere!

**Everything you need is available
in downloadable PDFs:**

- Set-up and game-play instructions

- Game master guide

- Answer sheets for players to fill in

- Clue cards

- Less-challenging word answer cards

- More-challenging pictogram answer cards

**To access these files, go to:
chrisgrabenstein.com/kids/
escape-from-mr-lemoncellos-library-game.php**

To get all the game pieces, you will need a user name
and a password. If you are a librarian or the person
organizing the game, just send an email to author@
ChrisGrabenstein.com, and Mr Lemoncello himself will
send you the two secret codes.

THE BOOKS, STORIES AND PERIODICALS IN
MR LEMONCELLO'S LIBRARY

(HOW MANY HAVE YOU READ?)

- ☐ *All-of-a-Kind Family* by Sydney Taylor
- ☐ *The American Heritage Dictionary of Idioms*
- ☐ *Anna to the Infinite Power* by Mildred Ames
- ☐ *Anne of Avonlea* by Lucy Maud Montgomery
- ☐ *Anne of Green Gables* by Lucy Maud Montgomery
- ☐ *Around the World in Eighty Days* by Jules Verne
- ☐ *Baby's Mother Goose: Pat-A-Cake*
- ☐ *The Brothers Karamazov* by Fyodor Dostoyevsky
- ☐ "The Cask of Amontillado" by Edgar Allan Poe
- ☐ *The Cat in the Hat* by Dr Seuss
- ☐ *Charlie and the Chocolate Factory* by Roald Dahl
- ☐ *Charlie and the Great Glass Elevator* by Roald Dahl
- ☐ *Coming Up for Air* by George Orwell
- ☐ *The Complete Sherlock Holmes* by Sir Arthur Conan Doyle
- ☐ *Crime and Punishment* by Fyodor Dostoyevsky
- ☐ *Cupcakes, Cookies & Pie, Oh, My!* by Karen Tack and Alan Richardson
- ☐ *Death on the Nile* by Agatha Christie
- ☐ *The Egypt Game* by Zilpha Keatley Snyder
- ☐ *Eight Cousins* by Louisa May Alcott
- ☐ *The Elevator Family* by Douglas Evans

☐ *The Eleventh Hour: A Curious Mystery* by Graeme Base
☐ *Even the Stars Look Lonesome* by Maya Angelou
☐ *Falling Up* by Shel Silverstein
☐ *From the Mixed-Up Files of Mrs Basil E. Frankweiler* by E. L. Konigsburg
☐ *The Giver* by Lois Lowry
☐ *Goodnight Moon* by Margaret Wise Brown
☐ *Great Day for Up* by Dr Seuss
☐ *Harry Potter and the Goblet of Fire* by J. K. Rowling
☐ *Harry Potter and the Philosopher's Stone* by J. K. Rowling
☐ *Huckleberry Finn* by Mark Twain
☐ *The Hunger Games* by Suzanne Collins
☐ *If I Grow Up* by Todd Strasser
☐ *I Love You, Stinky Face* by Lisa McCourt
☐ *Incident at Hawk's Hill* by Allan W. Eckert
☐ *In the Pocket: Johnny Unitas and Me* by Mike Leonetti
☐ *The Jungle Book* by Rudyard Kipling
☐ The King James Bible
☐ *Little House on the Prairie* by Laura Ingalls Wilder
☐ *Look Homeward, Angel* by Thomas Wolfe
☐ *Look, I Made a Hat* by Stephen Sondheim
☐ *Lord of the Rings* by J. R. R. Tolkien
☐ "The Masque of the Red Death" by Edgar Allan Poe
☐ *The Mousetrap* by Agatha Christie
☐ *Murder on the Orient Express* by Agatha Christie
☐ "The Murders in the Rue Morgue" by Edgar Allan Poe
☐ Nancy Drew: *The Mystery at Lilac Inn* by Carolyn Keene

- [ ] *The Napping House* by Audrey Wood
- [ ] *Nine Stories* by J. D. Salinger
- [ ] *No, David!* by David Shannon
- [ ] *Olivia* by Ian Falconer
- [ ] *One Fish Two Fish Red Fish Blue Fish* by Dr Seuss
- [ ] *Popular Science Monthly* magazine
- [ ] "The Purloined Letter" by Edgar Allan Poe
- [ ] *The Red Pyramid* by Rick Riordan
- [ ] *Scat* by Carl Hiaasen
- [ ] *Six Days of the Condor* by James Grady
- [ ] *Tales of a Fourth Grade Nothing* by Judy Blume
- [ ] *Ten Little Indians* by Agatha Christie
- [ ] *This Isn't What It Looks Like* by Pseudonymous Bosch
- [ ] *Through the Looking-Glass* by Lewis Carroll
- [ ] *Time* magazine
- [ ] *Treasure Island* by Robert Louis Stevenson
- [ ] *Turtle in Paradise* by Jennifer L. Holm
- [ ] *The Umpire Strikes Back* by Ron Luciano and David Fisher
- [ ] *Unreal!* by Paul Jennings
- [ ] *Up from Slavery* by Booker T. Washington
- [ ] *Walter the Farting Dog* by William Kotzwinkle and Glenn Murray
- [ ] *The Westing Game* by Ellen Raskin
- [ ] *When You Reach Me* by Rebecca Stead
- [ ] *Where the Sidewalk Ends* by Shel Silverstein
- [ ] *A Wrinkle in Time* by Madeleine L'Engle
- [ ] *The Yak Who Yelled Yuck* by Carol Pugliano-Martin

Books Sprinkled into
Mr Lemoncello's
Dialogue

- *Al Capone Does My Shirts* by Gennifer Choldenko
- *Alexander and the Terrible, Horrible, No Good, Very Bad Day* by Judith Viorst
- *Because of Winn-Dixie* by Kate DiCamillo
- *Bridge to Terabithia* by Katherine Paterson
- *Cloudy with a Chance of Meatballs* by Judi Barrett
- *Dead End in Norvelt* by Jack Gantos
- *Ella Enchanted* by Gail Carson Levine
- *The Essential Groucho,* edited by Stefan Kanfer
- *For Your Eyes Only* (James Bond) by Ian Fleming
- *Go, Dog. Go!* by P. D. Eastman
- *Great Expectations* by Charles Dickens
- *The Great Gilly Hopkins* by Katherine Paterson
- *Heart of a Samurai* by Margi Preus
- *I Can Read with My Eyes Shut!* by Dr Seuss
- *Joey Pigza Loses Control* by Jack Gantos
- *Maniac Magee* by Jerry Spinelli
- *Mrs Frisby and the Rats of NIMH* by Robert C. O'Brien
- *My Side of the Mountain* by Jean Craighead George
- *Oh, the Thinks You Can Think!* by Dr Seuss

- *The Phantom Tollbooth* by Norton Juster
- A Series of Unfortunate Events by Lemony Snicket
- *Something Wicked This Way Comes* by Ray Bradbury
- *Tuck Everlasting* by Natalie Babbitt
- *The Very Busy Spider* by Eric Carle
- *The Wind in the Willows* by Kenneth Grahame

READ ON FOR
A SNEAK PEEK . . .

Just about every kid in America wished they could be Kyle Keeley.

Especially when he zoomed across their TV screens as a flaming squirrel in a holiday commercial for Squirrel Squad Six, the hysterically crazy new Lemoncello video game.

Kyle's friends Akimi Hughes and Sierra Russell were also in that commercial. They thumbed controllers and tried to blast Kyle out of the sky. He dodged every rubber band, coconut custard pie, mud clod and wadded-up sock ball they flung his way.

It was awesome.

In the commercial for Mr Lemoncello's See Ya, Wouldn't Want to Be Ya board game, Kyle starred as the yellow pawn. His head became the bubble tip at the top of the playing piece. Kyle's buddy Miguel Fernandez was the green pawn. Kyle and Miguel slid around the life-size game like hockey pucks. When Miguel landed on the same square as Kyle, that meant Kyle's pawn had to be bumped back to the starting line.

"See ya!" shouted Miguel. "Wouldn't want to be ya!"

Kyle was yanked up off the ground by a hidden cable and hurled backwards, soaring above the board.

It was also awesome.

But Kyle's absolute favourite starring role was in the commercial for Mr Lemoncello's You Seriously Can't Say That game, where the object was to get your teammates to guess the word on your card without using any of the forbidden words listed on the same card.

Akimi, Sierra, Miguel and the perpetually perky Haley Daley sat on a circular couch and played the guessers. Kyle stood in front of them as the clue giver.

"Salsa," said Kyle.

"Nachos!" said Akimi.

A buzzer sounded. Akimi's guess was wrong.

Kyle tried again. "Horseradish sauce!"

"Something nobody ever eats," said Haley.

Another buzzer.

Kyle goofed up and said one of the forbidden words: "Ketchup!"

SPLAT! Fifty gallons of syrupy, goopy tomato sauce slimed him from above. It oozed down his face and dribbled off his ears.